# Diary of Sasha

# Written By Marita L. Kinney

Pure Thoughts Publishing, LLC

All Scripture quotation, unless otherwise indicated, are taken from the Holy Bible, New International Version®. NIV®. Copyright © 1973, 1978, 1984 by International Bible Society. Used by permission of Zondervan Publishing House.

**ISBN-13: 978-1492336211**

**ISBN-10: 1492336211**

# Dedication

This book was written for anyone who has ever felt defeated and may have lost their hope somewhere in their circumstance. There is someone right now who feels that life has treated them unfairly and seeks to hand their burden or to God, but cannot figure out a way to do so. This book is written for you. This book was written for me.

**Sasha**                                        **Marita Kinney**

## Contents

**Sasha**                                                    **Marita Kinney**

## Introduction
**Sasha**

"I know that you must think I'm crazy. But I have a lot to say and I haven't been given much time with you. I'm sure that you think that you know everything. Well, you don't know as much as you think you may. In fact, I'm certain that you have absolutely no idea what you're doing. A lot of you women are playing games with your lives and, to be perfectly honest, I don't have time to waste on you. But I pray that one of you will digest my words and feels my heart as I share my story with you. I used to be like some of you. Believe it or not, I was a 'hot commodity.' That's right. A lot of men used to desire me. Fact is, I could have had any man I wanted. They would do anything for me, anything. Soon I realized, however, that they were merely using me and I was guilty of using them. They would meet me and instantly undress me with their eyes; I could tell from their demeanor. I didn't mind being their eye candy either. At first it offended me, until the offense turned into a compliment. Every woman wants to feel desired. Every woman wants to feel admired. Right? See, I know. A lot of you are smiling and agreeing with me right now. I see you reminiscing. It's cool, but you see, those men had their agenda's and I had mine. I was trying to find a husband. While they were fantasizing about having sex with me, I was saying their last name in my head to see if it flowed well with my own name.

We were sizing each other up and had paid no attention to our incompatibility. I know what you're thinking, and no, this is not a love story. This is a story about how my life was taken from me and given back. I have two older sisters who seemed to live in another world. Their life was about church or earning money. I admired them and wanted some combination of their lives. I wanted a husband, money, and desired a relationship with God, as long as it didn't include going to church. The funny thing is I was doing everything wrong, trying to make everything right. I soon realized that the more I tried to fix my life, the more I messed it up. I had to hit rock bottom before I surrendered my life to God. I will begin by introducing myself. My name is Sasha, and this is my life…"

Sasha took a deep breath and closed her eyes gracefully.

## Chapter One

### Seventeen Years Earlier

**The Black Sheep Randi**

"I can't believe that she did that," Russell muttered as he walked into the bedroom to remove himself from the children's presence. Randi followed behind him with the intent of calming him down.

"Baby, you know how my sister can be. Please don't allow her to get to you like this," Randi said as she tried to defend her sister's behavior.

"What kind of woman is embarrassed of her family?" Russell asked rhetorically.

"Embarrassed? Baby, she's not embarrassed of us. Why would you say something like that? She just doesn't want any kids at her Grand Opening. I understand and it's not a big deal," Randi explained, hoping not to add fuel to the fire.

"You can think whatever you want to, Randi. Stacey is mean and hateful. She stays in our pockets and thinks that she can count our money. She assumed that we wouldn't be able to afford a babysitter. I personally don't want anything to do with her or her selfish ways. You're one of her biggest supporters and she didn't invite you to her Grand Opening because you have kids, who just happen to be her nieces and nephews. She didn't invite you because she thought you would bring the kids," Russell added, becoming more and more frustrated as he reflected on Stacey and how she belittled him and his family.

Randi touched his arm. "Baby, I understand your frustration; I really do. At the end of the day, Stacey is going to be Stacey. She's always been the way she is and I don't expect anything different from her."

"Sister or not, I'm not going to allow anyone to disrespect my wife," Russell fumed while he sat on the bed and began to remove his shoes.

"Aw baby, you're sticking up for me," Randi giggled, not bothered by her oldest sister's request. She sat down on the bed next to Russell and pulled his feet onto her lap. She dreaded her husband being upset and wanted to change his mood immediately. She began to massage his feet and remained silent as he continued to vent.

Randi's phone rang, interrupting Russell mid-sentence. She stopped what she was doing and walked towards her purse to retrieve her phone before the annoying ringtone sounded again. She was tempted to hit ignore, but noticed that it was her younger sister, Sasha. Knowing that Sasha was infamous for repeat calls, she decided against her better judgment just to answer the phone.

"Hello?!" Randi answered in her sarcastic enthusiastic voice.

"Hey, Boo! Are you going to Stacey's Grand Opening?" Sasha asked as she fumbled around in her make-up bag.

"No. I won't be attending her event tonight, but please send her my love," Randi replied.

"What? Why? Ok, I didn't think that you weren't actually going to be there,"
Sasha said, confused as to why her sister was not going. Sasha took a deep breath.

"Randi, why don't you want to go?" she asked, wanting a more detailed explanation.

"It's not that I didn't want to go. We just won't be going, Sasha, that's all. Please stop asking so many questions," Randi replied as she grew more and more frustrated, feeling rejected by her sister Stacey.

"That's not why, Randi. Tell her that you WEREN'T INVITED!" Russell yelled, hoping that Sasha would hear him in the background.

"Did he just say that you weren't invited? Oh h*.. no, I mean heck no Randi," Sasha said vehemently. She was disgusted that Stacey did not invite both of her sisters to the event.

"Calm down, Sasha before you keep cussing; it's cool,"

Randi explained.

"No, it's not cool, Randi. That's just trifling and please excuse me for cussing, but that's crazy and you know it," Sasha answered.

"YOU DON'T HAVE TO STOP CUSSING. SASHA, I THOUGHT I WAS ABOUT TO START CUSSING, TOO. BUT THANK GOD FOR THE HOLY GHOST!" Russell yelled from across the room as he began to laugh at himself.

"Tell Russell that I'm on the same page as he is," Sasha replied.

"Ya'll need to stop. It's all good," Randi said, not finding any humor in the controversial conversation regarding her oldest sister Stacey.

"Well, if you're ok with it then that's on you, Randi. However, I wish that she would do something scandalous like that to me. Shoot, I have a baby too."

Randi remained silent and kept her thoughts to herself.

"Since you're not going and obviously don't care, can you watch Tia for me?" Sasha asked, relieved that she had found a babysitter.

"That's probably why you called me in the first place, isn't it?" Randi guessed.

"No! Not at all, Boo," Sasha giggled.

"Yeah, right. Hurry up and bring her before I change my mind," Randi suggested. She began to laugh to keep from crying.

"Ok, you don't have to tell me twice. I'm on my way," Sasha answered and hung up the phone without saying good bye.

Randi looked down at the phone in disappointment, and then returned it to her purse. She felt Russell staring at her and dreaded what he had to say. She knew that he would definitely have something negative to say about Sasha dropping off her eighteen month old baby. He always frowned upon her parenting and didn't have much respect for her maternal instincts.

"What?" asked Randi, as Russell stared at her.

"Nothing, nothing. Actually, I do have something to say. Aren't you tired of your sisters treating you like crap? And then you wonder why I don't like being around them. I can't stand it, Randi. They make fun of your weight, make jokes about us having a big family, and Stacey treats us as if we're beneath her. We may not have a lot of money, but we're richer than they are. Stacey and Larry don't have a marriage, they have a business relationship. Can't you see that they're jealous of you, Randi? You're everything that they wish they could be," Russell lectured as he walked closer to Randi in compassion.

"Baby they're not jealous of me. They've treated me this way since before I can remember. It has nothing to do with our marriage, Russell. They treat me like the black sheep of the family because I'm not skinny and pretty like them. Russell, you were my first boyfriend..." Randi mumbled.

"Let me stop you right there. I know that they're your sisters, but baby, you are beyond pretty. You're beautiful and that's why I married you. God saved you just for me and protected you from men who would have scarred and abused you otherwise. Stacey and Sasha look up to you, even if they never admit it," Russell added while putting his arms around Randi's voluptuous waist.

Randi did not say another word. Instead, she rested in her husband's confidence in her. As Russell continued to embrace her, there was a knock at the door. Randi kissed Russell and headed towards the door. It was Sasha, and her niece Tia. With the cell phone glued to her ear, Sasha failed to speak to anyone. Sasha took off Tia's coat and continued her conversation with the person Randi assumed was Stacey. Randi ignored Sasha's rudeness and assisted Tia.

"Here," Sasha said, as she handed Randi her cell phone.

"Who is it?" asked Randi, pretending to be oblivious.

"It's Stacey," Sasha replied abruptly.

"Hello, Stacey," Randi answered in a charismatic tone.

"Please don't get on the phone as if you're delighted to

speak with me. Why would you tell Sasha that I didn't invite you to my Grand Opening?" Stacey asked, not holding back that she was highly offended.

"Well Stacey, I wasn't invited. Sasha got upset once she realized that I wasn't going. I'm perfectly fine," Randi explained as she rolled her eyes at Sasha and picked up her tired niece.

"First of all, I never thought that I had to invite you to anything. Randi, you're my sister and you should have known that you don't need an invitation. You got your feelings hurt for assuming. But whatever, Randi, it's so like you to play the victim. Although you weren't formally invited, I knew that your excuse would be that you didn't have a babysitter anyway," Stacey babbled.

"Stacey, that's also an assumption. I was never given an option to find a sitter. You failed to give me detailed information regarding your opening and assumed that I wouldn't have made it or you were afraid that I'd bring the kids," Randi replied.

"That wasn't the case, but you can think whatever you want. I'm inviting you now. If you can make it, that's great. I'm sure Russell will watch the kids for you. Oh, and if you decide to come, make sure you send me a picture of what you're going to wear," Stacey insisted.

"A picture of what I'm wearing?" Randi asked, to verify that she heard her correctly.

"Yes, a picture, because this is a classy event. You're my sister and you represent me. There is no way that I want you coming to my event looking like a hot mess," said Stacey.

Randi's heart became heavy and she could not utter a word. Politely, she handed the phone back to her baby sister, and walked away holding her niece, who had fallen asleep on her shoulder.

"Randi? Randi?" Sasha said. "I'm sorry." Randi continued to walk towards her bedroom, ignoring Sasha and trying to hold back her tears.

"RANDI!" Sasha yelled.

"THANKS, SASHA FOR RUNNING YOUR BIG MOUTH. I SAID THAT I WAS FINE!" Randi yelled as she opened her bedroom door and tears began to flow down her face instantly. Russell stood up with concern.

"You were right," Randi said as she laid Tia on her bed and dashed to the master bathroom to hide her sorrow.

"I was right about what?" Russell asked. "What's wrong, baby?"

"She's ashamed of me," Randi said through the bathroom door. Russell closed his eyes and took a deep breath. He hated seeing Randi so upset and there was nothing that he could do. She did not usually care what anyone thought of her, but when it came to her sisters, their words cut through her like a razor sharp blade.

**Sasha**                                                    **Marita Kinney**

Russell left the bedroom in anger and stormed down the hallway to confront Sasha for instigating. Before he could reach the living room, he heard Sasha slam the door. Deciding not to make matters worse, he chose not to follow her.

In the meantime, Randi removed her clothes slowly and ran herself a hot, soothing bubble bath. She stared at herself in disgust as she looked herself up and down in the oversized bathroom mirror. She ran her hands across her stretch marks and pulled on her unwanted belly fat, extending its elasticity. Randi then turned towards the tub, trying to dismiss the thoughts of drowning herself. She sat in the bathwater and watched it rise slowly. Her tears began to fall into the water like rain drops falling into a puddle in an abandoned alley. Her body disgusted her and was camouflaged by her fabricated smiles and pleasant demeanor. She was ashamed that, at thirty-six years of age, she had never learned to love herself.

## Chapter Two

**Sasha the Irresponsible Sister**

Sasha woke up and realized suddenly that she had overslept. Pulling the sheet up to cover her exposed breast, she glanced over at Lance, her "friend with benefits," with whom she sometimes hooked up to satisfy her sexual craving. She really liked Lance, but only pretended to agree with their casual sexual arrangement. Sasha wanted to be loved and yearned for a real relationship. She was pregnant with Tia when her last relationship ended on mutual terms. Sasha hated that Tia's father was sent to prison and she resented being a single mother. Lance seemed to be good for her, but was not very interested in Tia.

As Sasha continued to lie in bed, she imagined what life would be like with Lance. The more she pondered the fantasy, rather than feeling joy, she became more disappointed. Her good looks always seemed to bring her fleeting passions instead of love. She was desperate to change, but could not figure out what was wrong with her. She had thought for sure that she would be married by now.

"Good morning Lance!" Sasha cooed seductively, flirting with Lance as he began to open his eyes.

"Hey, Boo!" Lance answered groggily, not impressed by

Sasha's demeanor. Rubbing the sleep from the corners of his eyes, he sat up in bed.

"I have to leave to pick up Tia from my sister's house," Sasha said, realizing she had little time to do so before Randi left for church.

"I was wondering where little momma was," Lance replied, not convincing Sasha that he was genuinely concerned.

She began to get dressed and hoped that Lance would take the hint that he needed to leave. Without having to say a word, he began to get dressed as well, but with a noticeable attitude. Sasha knew that he wanted a quickie and did not care that she needed to leave. Further annoyed by his silent tantrum, Sasha stopped in the middle of getting dressed and gave Lance what he wanted. Feeling belittled and helpless, she gave herself to him once more. As usual, she felt conflicted with wanting to be desired and being able to recognize true love.

Meanwhile, at Russell and Randi's house.

"ANT ANT ANT ANT ANT...ANT ANT ANT."

"Randi, are you going to turn off that alarm clock?" Russell asked with his tooth brush hanging out of his month as he peeked his head around the bathroom door.

"Ok! I'm up, I'm up," Randi whined.

"Shhh! I've been up with Tia all night. Please don't wake up that child," Russell begged.

"Aww, look at you babe," Randi mumbled sleepily as she scooted Tia over, moving her closer to the middle of the bed.

"Don't 'aww' me. Babe, I'm tired," Russell laughed. "Sasha never called you back to say that she wasn't picking up Tia, did she?" Russell asked.

"Nope! You know how she is. I guess we'll just have to take Tia to church with us," Randi pointed out. "You know that I don't mind my Boo Boo Tia staying overnight, but Sasha has to do better. I called her four times last night and got no answer."

"I can't stand it when she does that. She's so inconsiderate," Russell said.

"Yes, I agree she's very inconsiderate. I understand that she's young and likes to party, but doing stuff like this is just disrespectful and irresponsible. Now I have to get five kids ready for church, stop by the store to get Tia some diapers, and figure out how everyone is going to fit into the van. Besides that, I don't have a car seat for Tia," said Randi.

"Babe, calm down. Go ahead and get ready for church. I'll

cook breakfast for the kids and run to the store. I also think we still have Carter's car seat up in the attic," Russell reassured her.

"Sounds like a plan," Randi stated and jumped up to get dressed.

"Before you wake up all the kids and get dressed, Mrs. Russell Wright, why don't you join me for some fellowship in the bathroom," Russell suggested with a seductive grin plastered on his face.

"You don't have to ask me twice," Randi exclaimed.

**Stacey the Money Hungry Sister**

At the same time, Stacey and her controlling husband, Larry, were not seeing eye-to-eye, and she had become emotionally drained by his alpha male, dominating, and selfish presence. After receiving numerous congratulations at her Grand Opening, she still yearned for Larry to acknowledge her accomplishment.

"Stacey, you're too soft. This is our money you're talking about. If that woman doesn't pay her rent by tomorrow, you need to evict her and that's the end of it. I don't care how *saved* she claims to be," Larry said sternly.

"You think that I enjoy people owing me money?" Stacey asked, but only further annoyed Larry, who often lost his cool when he was in his business mode.

"Well, then you need to do something about it. And now you've started another business. I'm trying to calculate how much money that's going to end up costing me. I want you to do well, but you have to get a backbone, Stacey. You can't allow people to take advantage of you. I can't stand being around weak people," he added.

"Are you serious? So, *I'm* weak now? And you actually think my business is going to fail before it has a chance to start. My real estate firm will not cost *you* a dime, I promise you that," Stacey replied, her heart dropping from his lack of support.

"Yeah, Ok. Let's see. You have your little sister owing you money cause she can't keep a job to pay you back. You rent a property to a member of the church and she's two months behind. But instead of accepting their money, you accept their excuses, Stacey! That spells weak to me," he said as he waited for Stacey's reply, but she remained quiet to try to defuse the tension.

"I understand Larry, and you're right. There are some things that need to change, but I need your support, not your criticism," she pleaded while she finished getting dressed for church. As she put together the final pieces of her outfit, she stepped into her walk-in closet to retrieve her favorite red bottom pumps, instantly adding five inches to her height.

"I hear you, darling. Actions speak louder than words and frankly, I'm done talking about this. Money is money. You either have it or you don't. And it remains obvious that you come from a family that doesn't. I'm not about to allow your bad money management to break me. That's why we have separate accounts. You'll learn sooner or later. Jerks get paid, nice guys soon fade," Larry added as he put on his custom made cuff links.

Stacey rolled her eyes discreetly in disagreement with Larry's comments.

"Are you ready for church?" she asked softly, hoping to change the subject.

"Go ahead, I'll be there if I can," Larry replied, as if he had other plans that did not include Sunday morning worship.

"Where are you going then?" Stacey asked, her forehead wrinkled with concern.

"I'm going to make *my* money. I'll be at my office finishing up a proposal for a new contract," Larry claimed without making eye contact with her, then laughed to himself.

"But you never go to the office on Sundays," Stacey stated.

"I do now," Larry replied as he kissed Stacey on the forehead and walked out their bedroom door. She stood in disbelief at how miserable she had become in her marriage. The reason why she had married Larry was the same reason that she had grown to resent him: money.

Stacey's vision blurred as she fought her tears. While tortured by Larry's words, which continued to replay in her thoughts, she heard the garage door open as he left their "home," which was no more than a place of shelter.

## Chapter Three

The spirit of God was in the building and the whole church was overwhelmed. The pastor did not have a chance to deliver the Word because the Holy Spirit had done all of the work. Randi and Russell stood side by side, hand in hand, giving all honor and praise to God. It was only a matter of time before Russell would understand how broken she actually was. Feeling rejected and alone, Randi let go of Russell's hand and walked up to the altar for prayer. Russell's eyes filled with tears watching the back of Randi's head as she approached the aisle. Randi did not normally go up for prayer. She was in rotation as an alter worker and it was not her Sunday to work. The timing could not have been better because she was the one standing in need of prayer. Russell continued to stand and watched all five children as they began to nod off.

Just as Randi returned to her seat, she noticed Sasha sneaking in the double doors wearing her dark shades. Randi ignored her feelings towards and disappointment with Sasha and continued towards her seat. Russell noticed Sasha too. He grabbed Randi's hand to assist her back to her seat. Walking past the pews, she seemed to annoy others around her and Russell knew how uncomfortable it made her. Feeling relieved and encouraged, Randi reached for Russell's hand for additional comfort.

Forty-five minutes later, church was finally dismissed.

Without hesitation, Sasha raced over towards Randi to pick up Tia.

"I didn't think that ya'll were going to be here," Sasha exclaimed.

"Well, hello to you too, Sasha, and why would you think that?" Randi asked flatly, not interested in any of Sasha's excuses.

"I just thought that since you had Tia last night you would have stayed home. Hey, baby girl," Sasha said as she hugged Tia and avoided eye contact with Randi. Russell said nothing. He packed up the other children, not wanting to interfere with their conversation.

"Babe, I'm going to take the kids to the van," he said as he noticed that Randi was about to address her concerns. He then walked away rapidly with the children.

"Ok, babe," Randi replied.

"Ugh, what's wrong with him?" Sasha asked, pushing her sunglasses on top of her head.

"What's wrong with *him*? Sasha, what's wrong with *you*? Why do you think that it's ok to leave Tia with me like that? You didn't answer your phone after I called you four times, you didn't leave Tia any clothes or diapers, and you're simply undeniably irresponsible. Do you realize how hard it is to get five kids ready for church?" Randi asked irritably.

"Why are you tripping? You decided to bring her to church

with you. I came by your house this morning to pick her up and ya'll were already gone. Besides, what's one more kid? You and Russell have a whole team of kids. If you don't want Tia to come over, then she won't. Also, about last night, my cell phone died, so I couldn't call you," Sasha replied, extremely annoyed.

"Of course I don't mind Tia coming over, but where were you last night? I'm sure that Stacey's Grand Opening didn't last all night," Randi said as her anger turned to concern. Sasha rolled her bloodshot eyes and refused to answer.

"Sasha, where were you?" Randi persisted.

"First of all, I'm a grownup, Randi. The last time I checked, our mother died three years ago," Sasha retorted.

"And the last time I checked, grown women inform their child's caregiver of their whereabouts just in case they're needed. Being twenty-eight does not make you a grownup," Randi stated.

"I went out," Sasha answered promptly. "Look, I have a hangover and I don't feel like being interrogated. I just came here to pick up Tia."

"Of course," Randi replied as she noticed Stacey walking towards them in her custom fitted suit and five inch heels.

"Excuse me. Sasha, can I speak with you when you get done here?" Stacey asked.

"Good morning, Stacey," Randi added.

"Really?" replied Stacey, as Sasha smirked.

"Randi, you did all those theatrics for what? To not even come to my Grand Opening anyway? Please get over your pity party, because that's something that you better not invite me to again," Stacey advised.

"Pity party? Sasha made a big deal out of nothing by calling you yesterday. I'm fine, Stacey," Randi reassured her.

"Whatever, Randi. I'm tired of your drama. You're always the victim and I don't have anything to say to you," Stacey replied.

"I understand," Randi said as she reached for her purse to get out a greeting card for Stacey. Sasha stood patiently. She watched Randi hand the card to Stacey and then felt bad as she watched her walk away.

"Don't feel sorry for her," Stacey said as she looked down at her manicured nails.

"I was just trying to help when I called. Stacey, she was exactly not the one who was upset, it was Russell and I. I thought that it was pretty messed up and that's why I called.

"Well, whatever. That's why I don't fool with y'all. It's always something and I don't have time to invest in matters that don't make me money. By the way, when are you going to get a job and start paying me back?" Stacey asked as the lights began to go off in the sanctuary.

"I have a job interview this week, so I'll be able to pay you back soon. I can't remember how much I even owe you," Sasha giggled, taking the matter lightly.

"Three thousand, eight hundred and seventy-five dollars, to be exact," Stacey replied with a straight face, reminding Sasha that her debt had not been forgotten.

Sasha was embarrassed. She did not realize that she owed her sister so much. She bit her bottom lip and looked worried.

"Look, I know it's a lot of money, but you need to make a payment arrangement or something. Larry was questioning me and you know how he is about money. I refuse to have my husband upset with me because you're irresponsible," Stacey said sternly.

"If I'm so irresponsible, why did you give me all that money?" asked Sasha.

"I'M LOCKING UP," one of the deacons yelled from the hallway.

"I'm still trying to figure that out," Stacey replied as she turned from Sasha and began to walk towards the lit EXIT sign, ending the conversation without even saying good bye to Sasha or her niece Tia.

# Chapter Four

The sound of Sasha's keys echoed through her apartment hallway as she unlocked her door. Annoyed that Tia had dropped her sippy cup, she sucked her teeth and gave her a death stare. At times she forgot how young Tia was and lost her patience easily due to her unrealistic expectations of a toddler. She knelt down to pick up the cup when she noticed a cell phone laying on the ground. It did not take long for her to realize that it was Lance's. She rushed Tia inside the house. Handing her the set of keys to occupy her, she sat her on the sofa. Sasha began to contemplate whether she was going to go through the phone. She turned the idea over and over in her mind. Her curiosity was growing, but she feared how Lance would react if he knew that she had snooped through his phone. As much as Sasha wanted to be nosey, she laid the cell phone down on the coffee table to suppress the temptation.

Suddenly realizing that it was time for Tia's snack, Sasha could not have been more overjoyed to get her mind off of Lance's phone. She placed Tia in her high chair, when out of the blue, the cell phone began to vibrate. The vibration magnified as it rattled against the glass coffee table. Sasha did not waste any time checking to see who was calling. A million thoughts ran through her mind. As she walked towards the phone, she wondered if it could be Lance calling to locate his phone. The phone stopped vibrating just as Sasha got to it. Disappointed that she missed the call, she paused and started to question whether she would have answered the phone anyway. With the thought that Lance could have called, she convinced herself that it was not unethical to look at his call log. As she began to maneuver her way through the abandoned cell phone, she could not help but notice that he had nineteen missed calls from someone named Tamera. Jealousy boiled throughout her body and Tia's hungry cries began to fade. She did not think that she and Lance were exclusive. However, she did assume that she had seen him enough that he would not need to deal with any other women.

Lance had always been so dominant over Sasha that she never felt comfortable enough to question him. Sasha keeping a tight lip was the norm, until Tamera popped up from out of nowhere. Now there was no holding back. Sasha began to initiate a full investigation to find out who Tamera was and why she felt comfortable enough to call Lance so many times. Although Sasha was angry, she felt relieved to know that Lance had chosen to spend the night with her instead of Tamera. Searching boldly through the cell phone, she went directly to Lance's text messages. Prepared to read his whole text history, she became frustrated when she discovered that all the messages had previously been deleted. Furious and hurt, she was determined to have her competition revealed. She was ready to size her up and do whatever she needed to do to in order to keep Lance's attention. Sasha could not seem to find anything relating specifically to

Tamera and was running out of options. The last resort was to call Tamera to find out all of the facts. Sasha continued to search through his phone and her stomach dropped when she noticed a picture of a woman in his gallery. She was pretty but in a plain way. The woman's style was the opposite of hers and she had small breasts. Sasha felt a bit insecure because she had always wanted a breast reduction, although Lance claimed to love her 36DD cup size. Seeing the pictures in the phone made Sasha want to discover Tamera's relationship with Lance even more. She wanted to intimidate the woman for her own satisfaction. She knew that calling Tamera might ruin everything between her and Lance, but decided that the truth was more important.

Tia was screaming now, which brought Sasha's investigation to a halt. The last thing that she wanted was to have a crying baby in the background when she made a call to another woman. Since she had made up her mind to call this Tamera, she memorized the number just in case Lance showed up to retrieve his phone. Minutes went by and it felt like an eternity as Sasha rushed to make Tia's lunch. With nothing prepared, Sasha dived into the pantry to get a loaf of bread. She could not undo the knot that she had tied previously, so she decided to rip the bag wide open. Just as she was about to make Tia a sandwich, she looked over and noticed that Tia had cried herself to sleep. Relieved, she tiptoed past the baby and grabbed the phone. Her palms began to sweat as she held the phone tensely. Sasha was barely in her bedroom when the cell phone began to vibrate again. She swallowed her spit and cleared her throat.

"Hello," Sasha answered.

"Um, who is this? Put Lance on the phone," Tamera commanded in a rage.

"You don't need to know who I am and why are you calling for Lance?" Sasha asked boldly.

"Look, I don't know who you are and I really don't care. I'm looking for my husband and I assume that you're the broad that he's been with all night."

"Your husband? Broad? You must be out of your mind. Lance isn't married and I don't have time to play these games with you," Sasha replied, but she was becoming confused.

"I don't know what Lance has told you, but he's a married man. A VERY MARRIED MAN. We have been married for nine years and we have three daughters together and a son on the way," the woman explained as she broke down and began to weep.

Sasha was speechless. She could tell from the conversation that the woman was telling the truth. Her legs started to shake uncontrollably as she stared at her unmade bed. The sheets were heavily scented with the aroma of sinful sex. Dried semen stains were smeared across her bed, making her nauseated. The woman continued to talk and pour out her heart, but Sasha could no longer hear her. The guilt was sucking the life out of her and she was struggling spiritually to breathe. She had to redeem herself and before the woman could stop talking, Sasha interrupted.

"Look lady, I'm terribly sorry. I had no idea that Lance was married," Sasha said as she massaged her temple.

"He's cheated on me before and women like you are a dime a dozen," replied the Tamera woman.

"*Excuse* me?" replied Sasha defensively. "Women like me? Look, Tamera, or whatever your name is. First of all, you don't know me. Don't blame your dysfunctional marriage on me. Lance has made a vow to you and he's to blame," Sasha said candidly.

"Well, if you actually knew who you were sleeping with, then maybe you would have known that he was indeed married. Just like I said. Women like you," the woman stated.

"Lady, you don't know me," Sasha repeated, her eyes filled with tears.

"You're wrong, I do know you. I may not know your name, but I know the spirit that operates in you. That's why all you women are the same. You'll lay down with anyone and don't know anything about them. Do you even know my husband's last name?" asked the woman.

Sasha sat and pondered the woman's statements. The more she reflected on the hurtful, yet true words that she spoke, the more she became offended.

"Women like me, huh. It's funny how *women like me* can take your man and not even know it. I didn't know that he was married and that's not my style. You don't have to be worried about him coming over here again. He's your problem, not mine," she said, bold again.

"Please don't be mistaken, Jezebel, you haven't taken my man. I still have a ring on my finger and he would never seriously consider being with a woman like you. As I said before, you're just like all the rest of those nasty women out there. You'll spread your legs for whoever wants to take a dive. My husband has his faults, but I'm a strong woman of God who's willing to pray for my man. Honey, you can't do anything for him. He's fighting a spiritual war and if he's not sleeping with you, then he's sleeping with someone else. It's always the same woman, different name," Tamera explained.

Sasha's rage grew; she felt betrayed by Lance on so many levels. She had mixed emotions. She felt like scum and yet was extremely annoyed by the woman's stereotypes of her. For the first time, Sasha was biting her tongue, yielding to the woman's pain and vulnerability. She was reaching her boiling point and did not know how much longer she would be able to keep her composure. The more she thought about what Lance had done to her, the more she wanted to hurt someone. The woman continued to talk until Sasha cut her off rudely.

**Sasha**                                    **Marita Kinney**

"OK, OK, OK! I get it! You think you know women like me. I'm sorry that you're going through this, sweetie, but I'm not the one to blame for all this drama. I understand that you're a Christian woman and all that, but stop blaming all of your husband's issues on him or me. I went through his phone and saw a pic of you and you're the typical, plain Jane Christian woman who has probably become boring to him…," Sasha stated before she was cut off in the middle of her sentence.

"EXCUSE ME!" the woman responded, outraged.

"No, I'm going to finish talking. I have the floor now. Church women like you are also a dime a dozen, Boo Boo. You're so consumed with church that you're probably neglecting your husband. While you're in Wednesday night Bible study, he's probably home alone, feeling like he's second place in your life. Your church schedule has allowed room for the enemy to enter into your home, dear. So, don't talk to me all deep about spirits and forget to mention that Satan can use the church as a distraction and divide couples in the process. Yes, you're saved, but not dead. What man wants to come home to someone who is dressed like his mom?" Sasha asked,  no longer feeling sorry for the woman.

"Is that what you think? Honey, my husband and I do make love. How do you think that I had my three daughters and got pregnant again?" the woman argued.

"Look, I know that you may be trying to be a good wife,

but the reason why these so- called church men cheat with women like me is simple. They want a sexy wife; they want you to say things to them that you wouldn't dare say to anyone else. They want a fantasy. That's why a lot of men crave porn. Your husband pursued me," Sasha explained frankly. "I could teach you what he likes." Sasha laughed at the idea of offering bedroom tips.

"Since you're an expert on marriage, why aren't you married?" the woman asked. This was a low blow to Sasha, as that was exactly what she wanted to be. She did not understand why no one had offered to marry her yet. She had been with a lot of men, but realized that something was missing. She was beautiful, had a great shape, knew how to please a man, but questioned if she was actually suited to be a wife.

Sasha took a long pause before answering. The other woman knew that she had hit a nerve.

"When Lance comes home to you, tell him to forget that he ever knew me. You can also tell him that he'll need to file a claim to replace his cell phone, because it will accidently be dropped into the toilet along with all of his lies and bull," Sasha stated as she hung up, began to rip all the sheets from her bed and threw the cell phone at the wall as hard as she could. She then gathered the sheets and headed towards the bathroom, where she threw the sheets into the tub. Next she ran down the hallway and grabbed the bleach from her linen closet. Without hesitation, she poured the whole bottle of bleach on the sheets as if she could wash the sin of adultery away. The bleach splashed everywhere and started to discolor the shower curtain. Tears streamed down her face like a leaky faucet. Saddened at the thought that Lance had stolen, and then broken her heart, she realized suddenly that she was desperate to be loved. The reality was that she gave her heart away to anyone who could manipulate it just enough to make her feel good in the moment.

## Chapter Five

KNOCK. KNOCK. KNOCK.

Sasha got up, looked through her peephole and discovered that Randi was standing at her door. Although she did not feel like having company, she knew that she had to apologize for leaving Tia with her the week before. She opened the door and gave Randi a nonchalant greeting.

"Well, good day to you too, Boo."

"Hello, Randi."

"Dang, you act as if speaking to me is going to kill you. I'm not mad at you, Sasha. What happened between us is over. Girl, you know that I don't hold grudges."

"I know, but I feel terrible about what I did. You were right. I'm irresponsible," Sasha admitted.

Randi could not believe her ears. She was shocked that Sasha actually admitted that she was irresponsible.

"Wow, that was very mature of you. Is everything ok?" Randi said jokingly, but Sasha did not laugh. It was not like Sasha to be the serious sister and not have a smart aleck comeback.

"I got the job that I interviewed for."

"That's awesome, but why are you changing the subject?"

**Sasha**                                    **Marita Kinney**

Sasha rolled her eyes and knew that Randi was not going to let up until she got some answers. Randi had become like a second mother to her and was way less judgmental than Stacey. She was torn over Lance and needed someone to confide in.

"I've been going through a lot and haven't felt like talking to anyone."

"You feel like talking about it now? You look so depressed."

Sasha began to cry as she thought about her latest scandal.

"Randi, I can't believe that you came out of the house dressed like that?"

"What? Where did that come from?"

"I'm just tired of seeing you look like an old maid."

"Why are you and Stacey so concerned with the way I dress? Your rude comments are getting on my last nerve and you two have absolutely no regard for my feelings."

"Stop being so sensitive. I'm just concerned because you're married and need to keep Russell looking only at you."

"Excuse me? What makes you think that my husband has stopped looking at me? You're way out of line, Sasha. What's wrong with you?"

Sasha dropped her head in shame and replied, "I slept with

a married man."

"Who?"

"Oh, no. He's no one you know."

"Ok, dear, I just wanted to get that straight first."

"This guy I was seeing."

Randi did not say a word and knew that there had to be more to the story, or at least hoped so. She knew Sasha could be promiscuous at times, but never considered her to be a home wrecker.

"He played me. He never told me that he was married. I can't believe that I didn't know."

"What do you mean you didn't know? How could you not know, Sasha?"

"First of all, he didn't wear a wedding ring. He actually didn't seem like the husband type. Plus, he came to see me all the time.

Randi stared at Sasha in disgust.

"I never thought to ask him. I immediately assumed he was single."

"Have you ever been to his house?"

"No."

"Have you ever seen him during regular hours? I'm not talking about late night creeping. Have you ever consistently seen him during daytime or early evening hours?

"No."

"Sasha, that's enough right there to make a woman skeptical."

Sasha was overwhelmed with disappointment and avoided eye contact with Randi. She was humiliated. She buried her face in her hands and began to sob.

Randy ceased to interrogate her. It was obvious that Sasha was remorseful and just needed her sister to comfort her without any judgment.

"Please don't tell Stacey about this."

"Why would I do that?"

"Because she asked me about him all the time, probably because I told her that he was an attorney."

"You told her about him and told her about his career? Of course she's going to ask about him. What were you thinking? Stacey stays in your business because you put her in your business."

Sasha sat and thought about what Randi said.

"I was so stupid," Sasha replied, as she reminisced about

her love affair with Lance.

"I hate that you have to go through this, but imagine how his wife must feel. I promise you that her pain is ten times worse than yours. That's if she ever finds out…"

"She knows."

"What?"

"He left his phone over here and she kept calling…so I answered."

"Oh my goodness," Randi said, her eyes open wide in shock and disbelief.

"That's when I found out he was married. I felt like a cheap whore talking to his wife. What makes it so bad is that I answered the phone like she owed me an explanation for calling my man's phone. You know how my mouth can be. I even called her by her name. I messed up big time Randi."

Randi began to sympathize with both Sasha and the other woman. Her heart became heavy and she began to pray silently, but loudly and boldly in her spirit. Sasha shook her head from side to side, both eyes closed tightly as if she was trying to awaken from a bad dream. There were no words that could comfort Sasha, so Randi just hugged her and they began to sob together.

## Chapter Six

Randi returned home having had a true wake up call. The conversation with Sasha was very fresh in her mind and she started to reevaluate her own marriage. She began to brainstorm about areas in which she could improve. Although she felt like she had a healthy marriage, she knew that it needed some maintenance and began to fear the worst case scenario. Russell was not back from taking the boys to the movies for their monthly father and son outing. He had done so religiously for two years and Randi looked forward to her kid free Sunday afternoon. With nothing to do, she had decided to visit Sasha to smooth things over, but came home devastated and paranoid. Sasha planted a seed of fear in her that never existed before and it grew, faster than any seed she knew of.

Frustrated and even more insecure with her image, she knew that Sasha was right. She began to wonder what if Russell admired other women from afar. With little time to waste, Randi made up her mind that she was going to live life differently. She refused to waste time with the excuse that she still had her baby weight; the truth was that her youngest child was five and that she had been neglecting herself terribly. Reality had hit her in the face, thanks to Sasha's drama, and she refused to neglect herself any further. She dashed to the bedroom and opened her undergarment drawer. She searched for a sexy pair of panties, but seemed to grab nothing that did not look like her period panties. No longer in denial, she knew that she was in desperate need of a makeover and knew just the person to call: "Stacey," she said aloud. Sucking up her pride, she took a deep breath, reached inside her coat pocket and took out her cell phone. Butterflies jittered around in her stomach, making it hard to place the call. She hurried to press send before she chickened out. The phone began to ring as she prayed that she would be sent to voicemail to avoid going through with her call.

"Hello?" Stacey answered brusquely.

"Hey Stacey, what are you doing?"

"What do you want, Randi? And no, I wasn't at church today, if that's why you're calling me."

"Actually, I was calling to talk to you. Believe it or not, I'm not your personal church patrol," Randi giggled, letting out a sigh to relieve some of her nerves.

"Well, this is a surprise. What's wrong?"

"Why does something have to be wrong for me to call my dear sister?"

"Ok, now you're terrifying me. You never call me for no reason."

"You're right! I was calling to tell you that you were right."

"Right about what."

"About everything."

"Shut the front door and where is my sister? I have no idea what you're referring to, but I like the fact that you're admitting that I'm right about something," Stacey exclaimed, grinning from ear to ear.

"I'm not going to lie. I was hurt when you asked me to send you a picture of what I was going to wear to your Grand Opening. I was hurt about a lot of things. Sometimes I think you're embarrassed of me and my children. That's why Russell is so cold towards you. I act like nothing you and Sasha do or say bothers me, but he has to see my tears and he can't stand to see me hurt," Randi admitted as she poured out her feelings.

"I can't believe that you actually thought that I was embarrassed of you and the kids. For the record, I'm not embarrassed of y'all. I just wish that you and I could have some grown up sister time together. You always have the kids with you and sometimes I need to vent without censoring my conversation. You're so sensitive and take things the wrong way. Personally, I hate rejection too, and every time that I ask you to do something, you always decline because of your family. Trust me, I get it. I just get angry because I miss having my sister around."

"Wow, I never thought about it like that. That means a lot to me. I had no idea that you felt that way. Well then, what about my appearance? Are you ashamed of me?"

"No."

"That's it, 'no'?"

"No, I'm not ashamed of you. I think you're beautiful. I just wish that you could see that. Sometimes you act like you don't care about yourself and that's what upsets me. I know that I don't say things as gently as you would, which could make me seem as if I'm being mean or rude. My intentions were never to hurt you. I just get so tired of seeing you put everyone before you. You let yourself go."

"I know," Randi mumbled, barely above a whisper. "That's why I called you, because I know that I could do better. I just don't know where to start."

"The fact that you want to change is a start."

"I agree, and that's why I called you. I want you to go shopping with me."

"OFCOURSE I'LL GO!" Stacey screamed in excitement. "This is going to be so much fun. You deserve a makeover. When do you want to go?"

"Well, Russell and the boys are still out. Are you available today?"

"It's a date. Meet me at the mall in forty-five minutes."

"Yes, ma'am. Oh… and I love you, Stacey."

"I love you too."

Stacey hung up the phone, overjoyed. She could not believe that Randi truly wanted a makeover. With only minutes to spare, she went into the living room to share her exciting news with Larry. As she approached the living room she could smell the fresh popcorn that Larry was eating.

"Babe! You're not going to believe this."

"What?"

"Randi called me and she wants to go shopping."

"Ok...and...?"

"Honey, that's a big deal. You know that we never go shopping together."

"I don't know what ya'll do together; I'm usually at work."

"Ok, I'm usually at work too, and you know that we never go shopping. What's wrong with you and why are you being so short?" Stacey asked, realizing that Larry was in one of his spontaneous bad moods.

"Look. Have fun with your sister. I'm trying to watch the game."

"Forget your game."

"What did you say to me?" asked Larry as he stood up from the couch, walked towards Stacey, and poured his popcorn on top of her head. Stacey squinted her eyes in rage and flared her nostrils.

"Oh, so I guess you're mad," Larry said as he raised his hand above his head to smack Stacey. She flinched and put her arms in front of her face to resist the impact. But he did not follow through. Seeing Stacey intimidated and crying instantly made him laugh hysterically.

"I'm not going to hit you. Go have fun with your sister."

Stacey turned and began to walk towards the downstairs guest bathroom. She brushed the popcorn out of her hair, picked her purse up from the floor and began to search for her makeup bag.

"Yeah, make sure that you get yourself together before you leave this house. Remember, you represent me," Larry emphasized as he watched Stacey walk into the bathroom.

## Chapter Seven

Randi waited patiently for Stacey at the food court and began to wonder if she had stood her up. Just as she was about to leave, she spotted Stacey walking towards her as the crowd from the smoothie line cleared. With a huge smile on her face, she met Stacey in the middle of the food court.

"Thank you so much for meeting me here on such short notice."

"No problem, I wasn't doing anything."

"What? You mean that you were actually at home relaxing and weren't working."

Stacey laughed because she worked just as much as Larry. Not because she was a workaholic, but because she just hated it when Larry rubbed his money in her face.

"Let's leave my work at work," Stacey said as she adjusted the shoulder strap of her purse.

"Done. So where should we go first?"

"What do you want to change?"

"Everything," Randi said with a nervous laugh to cover up her embarrassment. "I want to reinvent myself. I mean a huge change."

"Girl, what are you up to? How huge are we talking?" Stacey looked surprised and confused. She did not know if she should be happy or worried about Randi.

"I want to wear thongs kind of change."

"Huh? Are you ok? Not my conservative sister. You want to wear thongs? Girl, bye."

Stacey could not stop laughing. She could not believe her ears for one moment. As she opened her eyes, she looked at Randi's serious demeanor. "Sorry girl, but I really needed that laugh. So you really want to change everything about yourself? Why?"

"I'm tired of looking old. I still want to be conservative, but with some style. I want to wow my husband. I want to be sexy."

"Girl, you cannot buy sexy. Believe me when I tell you, Russell already thinks you're sexy. Don't pull me into your 'tramp stamp' makeover."

"My what?" Randi laughed.

"Randi, I agree that you need a major makeover. However you still need to be *you*. When I see you I don't think of thongs, honey."

"Well, you're wrong. How in the world did you think that I got all my children? I have some sexy clothes. I just think that it's time to step up my game. I don't want to become predictable. It's

time that I give Russell a new wife, a better wife, and a better me."
Randi became emotional and Stacey realized her sincerity. "I'm on
a budget, so I need to make small changes first," stated Randi.

"Don't worry about the money. This is on me. You deserve
it, Randi, and this is my gift to you."

"Are you serious?" Randi asked to confirm that she
understood Stacey correctly.

"Yes, I'm serious, and since you don't know where to start,
let's go to 'Victoria's Secret' first."

"'Victoria's Secret'?"

"Yes, honey! You need to feel sexy. Feeling sexy will help
you with your confidence. There is nothing about you that says
sexy right now. All I see is Mommy. You need to switch that to
Mami."

Randi blushed, but knew that Stacey was right and trusted
her advice.

"First, we're going to change your undergarments, then
your shoes, your clothes, and then I'll schedule an appointment for
your hair. No, scratch the hair appointment, I'll just call Sasha.
Besides, she owes me money anyway; she'll do it."

"Stacey, slow down. I don't have time to do all of this
today. Not to mention the mall closes in two hours."

"So I guess we better hurry up," Stacey suggested as she grabbed Randi's hand to hurry her along.

A couple of hours passed and Stacey had kept her word. She paid a total of twenty-six thousand dollars for Randi's makeover. The more Stacey swiped her credit card the more uneasy Randi felt. Although shopping carelessly was fun, Randi had a bad feeling about the amount of money that Stacey was spending.

"Stacey, I know that you offered to pay for all this stuff, but I'm not going to let you pay for everything."

"Randi, it's ok," Stacey reassured her as she thought about hurting Larry the only way that she knew how.

"I appreciate it, but my husband is not going to be ok with you spending all this money on me."

"Girl, bye. I'm your sister and he should be ok with me doing whatever I want to do for you. Just tell him that it's a late birthday present."

"No. I'm not lying to him."

"Ok, well I'm telling you right now that this is your late birthday present," Stacey replied with a genuine smile.

"I really appreciate that, but I really have decided to lose weight as part of my transformation. I may not be able to fit into these clothes in a few months."

"Well then, I guess we'll have a reason to go shopping again," Stacey grinned.

Randi saw Stacey in a light that she hadn't seen her in for years. For once, something seemed important to her other than work and money. It made her feel special that Stacey was looking forward to hanging out with her again. Then from out of nowhere, her cell phone began to ring. She expected it to be Russell, but was surprised to see that it was Sasha.

"Hold on, it's Sasha," Randi announced as she held her index finger up in the air, excusing herself from the conversation.

"Hello!"

"Hey, Randi. I forgot to ask you something when you were here."

"Oh? What's up?"

"You know that I just got that job and start tomorrow."

"Yes," Randi nodded.

"Well, I need a sitter. I wasn't expecting to start so soon. I don't have childcare lined up yet."

"What happed to that childcare center Tia was going to a few months ago?"

"They were too expensive and I owe them a balance."

"Ok, so you're calling me for…"

"Well, I was going to see if you could keep Tia for me."

"Are you serious? I love my niece, but you're not about to use me again, especially after the stunt you just pulled."

"I thought that you weren't mad at me."

"I'm not mad at you. I just learned that I can't trust you. Sasha you have to learn how to stand on your own two feet. That means that you can't continue to mistreat people for your own selfish needs. You burn bridges everywhere you go."

"I hear you, but I really need this job. Can't you just watch her until I get some childcare? It should only take a week or so."

"I can't do it, Sasha. I also have other commitments."

"Whatever, Randi, like what?"

"I'm in charge of a ministry at church during the day."

"Why can't Tia go with you?" Sasha asked sulkily.

"No Sasha, I can't. I'm sure that you'll find a sitter."

Before Randi could say "bye," Sasha hung up on her. Randi was not surprised that Sasha's mood had changed back to being nasty and disrespectful as soon as she did not get her way.

"She hung up on me."

"What's she pouting about this time?"

"She asked me to watch Tia for her and I said 'no'."

"Oh, Lawd, this is her calling me right now," Stacey announced as she answered the phone.

"Hello," Stacey answered calmly.

"Stacey, I got the job that I interviewed for."

"Really! Congrats, sweetie. You know that I'm happy for you. Now you can pay me back."

"I'm going to pay you back. I promise. The only problem I have is that I can't find childcare that I can afford."

"I see where you're going with this."

"I was wondering if you could help me with half the childcare expenses," Sasha suggested with a tone of entitlement.

"Girl, now I know you've lost your mind. Larry isn't going to go for that. That's why we don't have any children now. The last thing we want to do is pay for childcare. I'm sorry, sweetie, but I can't help you with that."

"Well then, can I borrow about five hundred dollars to pay my back balance?"

"You already owe me close to four thousand dollars—three thousand, eight hundred and seventy-five dollars to be exact, and now you're asking for more money? You're tapped out," Stacey lectured her.

"Whatever. I'll figure something out. Trust me when I tell

you, I can't wait to pay you back every dime."

"That's great to hear, Sasha. I look forward to it," Stacey said sarcastically as she hung up the phone.

She folded her arms and sighed.

"Why is it that when people owe you money, they get an attitude whenever you refuse to loan them more?" Sasha asked rhetorically.

"Exactly! Or why do people get an attitude if you no longer offer to babysit for them because they don't pick their kid up until days later. Not to mention, don't even call to say 'I'm going to be late,' 'kiss my butt,' or anything," Randi laughed.

"I'm happy that Sasha found a job, but she has to learn how to be responsible, point, blank, period. I will not enable her any longer."

"We're on the same page. I'm tired of her using me and taking my kindness for granted."

"Aren't there some sort of services that can help her?" Stacey asked.

"Yes. She used to get assistance for childcare but lost her benefits."

"What? How did she lose her benefits?" Stacey asked, curling her upper lip. "She needs all the help she can get. I take that back, she's more than capable of helping herself."

"She was leaving Tia there all day and it wasn't working. I guess someone reported her."

"She was probably laid up with some bum," added Stacey.

Randi nodded her head in agreement and knew exactly who Sasha had been seeing.

## Chapter Eight

Sasha hung up the phone; she was frantic. Feeling rejected by her sisters, she was desperate to find childcare before the next day. She was sure to be fired if she had to call in sick on the day of orientation. Although she made amends with Randi, it never crossed her mind that she could not count on her for help again. She had to do something and quick. Staying upset with her sisters was not going to help her find childcare. With no time to waste, Sasha began to look through her phone and call any and everyone that she felt could help her with Tia.

After making over a dozen phone calls, Sasha still had not found a sitter. Everyone whom she called was either too expensive, had no openings, or was closed for the weekend. Sasha glanced at Tia as she sat in front of the television occupied with a Dora DVD that she had watched several times already. Feeling helpless and discouraged, she began to think of all the excuses that she could tell her new boss in the morning. The more she tried to come up with a lie, the more she began to feel like a failure. At the end of her rope, she began to look through her contacts just one last time.

For Sasha, reality was finally setting in. She hated the way that people had started to perceive her. Half the people that she had called did not answer and the other half did not care to help her. Convinced that a job was the answer to all of her problems and determined to get herself out of debt, she needed to be at that job in the morning. She owed more student loans than she could remember and her job search was difficult because she had not obtained a college degree. The idea of attending college pleased her at first. However, without the motivation to go along with it, it became more of a burden and she was embarrassed that after six years of college, she did not even have an associate's degree. Sasha was hopeful that life had more to offer than what she had already received.

Just as she began to look through her contacts again, she received an incoming call from her partying buddy, Christina. Sasha perked up, knowing that Christina had two children and must know about other babysitters.

"Hey, Trick!" Sasha answered enthusiastically, greeting her friend in their normal manner.

"Hey, Miss Lady! What are you doing?" Christina asked.

"I was just sitting here going through my phone, trying to find a babysitter."

"A babysitter for what? There's nothing going on tonight," Christina implied.

"For my job."

"Since when did you get a job?"

"Well, it's for a temp agency. But anyway, it's something."

"I know that's right," Christina replied.

"Who do you use for childcare?"

"My momma keeps my kids for me. But I do know someone who watches kids."

"How much does she charge?" Sasha asked.

"I think she charges around seventy-five dollars a week."

"FOREAL! Girl, I need her number. Because I have called all these other places and they are trying to charge me almost two hundred dollars a week. My last name is not Jones, and I'm not trying to keep up with them," Sasha exclaimed as she took off her bra and pulled it through the sleeve of her shirt to get comfortable.

"Yes, girl, I know. I'm going to text you her number and just tell her that I sent you. Her name is Miss Susie."

"Ok, girl! Text it to me now so that I can call her right away. I start my job tomorrow."

"Ok, call me later," Christina replied.

"Sure thing. Thanks so much, Tina."

"No problem," Christina answered then hung up.

Sasha stood up and danced around the coffee table. Then suddenly she heard her phone chirp, alerting her that she had a new text message. She called the number immediately. As the phone rang, her anticipation grew.

"Hello?"

"Hello, my name is Sasha and I received your number from my friend Christina. She told me that you offer childcare."

"Yes, I do. How many children do you have?"

"I have one daughter."

"Ok, honey. How old is she?"

"She's eighteen months."

"Alright, sweetie. Well, I charge seventy-five dollars a week and also provide meals. I only watch kids Monday through Friday, from 7am to 6pm. Do those times work for you?"

"Yes, ma'am."

"You're more than welcome to come by my house to see how I operate here."

"Well, that would be great, but I start my job tomorrow morning and need childcare right away."

"Ok, honey, I understand. You can start bringing her tomorrow if you'd like."

"Really?"

"Sure, sweetie. I've been watching kids for over twenty years," Miss Susie stated proudly.

"That's great. Thank you so much for watching Tia on such

short notice."

"Pardon me, who?" asked Miss Susie.

"Tia. My daughter's name is Tia."

"Oh, ok. I wasn't sure what you said," Miss Susie laughed.

Sasha laughed along with her and felt relieved to have finally found a babysitter. Miss Susie continued on and then gave Sasha her address and directions. The conversation ended, leaving Sasha extremely excited about her new babysitter. She picked up Tia and began to give her Eskimo kisses. All of her worries seemed to have vanished in an instant and her evening of peace and quiet was looking promising. With the new job on her mind, Sasha began to prepare for her new workday. She was no stranger to procrastination and she wanted to do everything that she could to keep from being late the next day.

## Chapter Nine

It was bright and early and Sasha had arrived in front of her new babysitter's house right on time. Feeling good and professionally dressed, she got out of the car confidently and unstrapped Tia from her car seat. She placed Tia's feet on the street and held her tiny hand as they walked towards the front door to Miss Susie's house. After just one knock a beautiful woman with salt and pepper hair opened the door and let them in.

"Well, this must be Tia!"

"Yes, ma'am, and I'm Sasha. I called you last night."

"Of course, dear. Come in. Have a seat," Miss Susie offered. "So, before you leave, do you have any questions for me?" Miss Susie asked as she smiled and exposed her missing teeth.

"Not really. Oh yes, actually I do. Exactly how many kids do you watch during the day?"

"Right now, Tia will be my only child. The other children have just gone to kindergarten. A couple of my former kids have siblings on the way and I'll be keeping those babies when their mothers go back to work.

"Oh, ok. Well, thank you again for agreeing to keep her. I'll be back to pick her up around 5:30," Sasha stated as she stood up and began to walk towards the door. Tia seemed to be comfortable with Miss Susie until Sasha was about to walk out the door. Then she began to scream. Sasha's heart melted as she heard Tia's crying increase.

"She'll be fine. Go ahead on to work," Miss Susie exclaimed as she scooted Sasha on her way.

Sasha walked away feeling relieved that she had found someone to look after Tia so that she would arrive at her new job a couple minutes early. Although it was a temp position through her agency, she remained hopeful that if she performed well, she could be hired on fulltime. Motivated and excited, she pulled into the MacDonald's drive through to order a cup of coffee for her morning commute. As she rolled down her car window to place the order, the morning breeze filled the air. Sasha's attitude towards life was beginning to change and she was happy that she did not have to rely on her sisters after all. Just as the cashier took her money she looked at her phone as it began to vibrate in her lap. Startled, she grabbed the phone immediately to see who was calling her so early.

*I hope this isn't the babysitter,* she thought. However, it was an unexpected surprise instead. It was Lance. *I should answer the phone and cuss him out.* Instead of giving in to the urge to argue with him and getting into a bad mood, Sasha rolled her eyes and pressed ignore to dismiss his call. She had not heard from him or his wife since the day that she found out he was married. Lance did not even come back to look for the cell phone that he had left at Sasha's house. Sasha grinned as she reminisced about breaking the phone. She sipped on her coffee and turned on a morning radio show to shift her thoughts. Lance was the last person that she wanted to think about and she refused to waste any of her energy on him.

As she pulled into the company's parking lot, her stomach started to bubble and her nerves ran wild. She found a nearby parking spot and reapplied her lipstick. She was looking her best and was confident that she would impress her new boss and co-workers. Her long weekend was behind her and she could see nothing but her future. As she opened the door, the feeling of success smacked her in the face. She was mesmerized by the main lobby and could see herself walking into work there daily. She skimmed her tongue over her teeth a final time, making sure that no lipstick had gotten on them. Adjusting her skirt and sticking out her chest, she approached the front desk.

"Good morning? How can I help you?" the receptionist asked pleasantly.

"My name is Sasha and today is my first day."

"Great! Follow me and I'll take you to the orientation room."

Sasha followed the young receptionist and began to size her up without any effort or thought. The receptionist opened the door and there were several people waiting inside the room. Sasha entered and took the seat nearest to the door. She glanced around the room, crossed her legs, and waited for her new supervisor to arrive. The door finally opened and the newly-hired people put a halt to their awkward icebreaker conversations. An extremely handsome man entered the room and Sasha gave him her undivided attention. She was not sure if he was a new hire or her supervisor.

"Hello, and good morning, everyone. My name is Seth and I will be passing around your new hire paperwork. If you are with a temp agency, you won't need to fill out this packet. If you want some coffee or need to use the restroom, please feel free to do so at this time," the neatly dressed man instructed.

Sasha was still uncertain who Seth was to her exactly, but she was intoxicated by the scent of his cologne as he passed her. She tried to avoid eye contact with him, but the attraction was so thick in the air that she almost felt it. There was no denying that Seth was interested in her as well.

As Seth passed out the packets, Sasha glanced at his left hand to see if he was wearing a ring. The last thing that she needed was to have another married man end up in her life and her bed. Dealing with Lance made her more aware of the deceit that came along with dating. She was determined not to waste her time on another man who had nothing to offer her. Her heart was still broken and she knew that she was very vulnerable. Flirting with Seth was not appropriate, but she had to make a move. Whenever

## Sasha Marita Kinney

Sasha wanted something, she got it. And she felt a strong desire to get to know Seth on a more personal level. Sasha had a weakness for a lot of men and she did not doubt that she could have Seth too.

Workplace romance was never her cup of tea, but the unspoken body language between her and Seth was undeniable. Sasha knew that she was extremely sexy and that the other women in the orientation who were also attracted to Seth envied her. Competition was never her thing, because she never felt like she had any. Realizing that she slept with another woman's husband fed her ego and the shame that she felt turned into cockiness. Sasha found herself daydreaming in class about being with Seth. She imagined him with Tia if they were an item. The more she imagined it, the more she wanted to see if that could be made a reality. Time was flying by and it was almost the end of the day. She made it known during orientation that she was not interested in mingling with the other co-workers, but was interested solely in Seth. The day finally ended when Seth decided to let everyone leave early. The room filled with laughter as people exited. Meanwhile, Sasha pretended to be preoccupied in order to be the last person to leave.

"So, Sa...sha, is it?" Seth asked as he looked down at the name tag stuck on her chest.

"I like the way you say my name," Sasha replied, flirting with only her eyes and voice.

"Is that right? Well Sasha, it's a pleasure to have you. I hope that you enjoy working here. Let me know if there's anything that I can help you with."

"Thank you, Seth. I really appreciate that. And yes, there is something that you can do for me," Sasha told him.

"Really? What would that be?" Seth asked, curious to know what Sasha was going to say.

"You can wear that cologne again. It smells really nice and I concentrate better when I have a pleasant fragrance around me," Sasha giggled.

"Is that so? Well, I definitely want you to be focused, so I'll see what I can do." Seth grinned and walked out of the room.

Sasha was excited about work and could not wait to see Seth again. She did not intend to sleep with every man who was interested in her, but could not pass one up either. As she got into her car, she began to have mixed emotions. She really wanted to see Seth again, but knew that men had always been her weakness. Reality started to set in and Sasha knew that being with a man at her job could be a huge mistake. Still hurt by Lance's betrayal and wanting to forget him altogether, Sasha became convinced that Seth would shift her focus. Thoughts of Seth continued to fill her head as she drove back to the babysitter's house to pick up Tia. Time flew by and before she knew it, she had arrived.

**Sasha**                                        **Marita Kinney**

## Chapter Ten

The candle lit up the room as Sasha relaxed and lay on top of her pillow-top mattress reading her favorite book. She had finally gotten Tia to sleep and was tired from folding laundry. As she turned the page to her book, her phone began to ring. She was in a good mood and did not want her evening to be interrupted with any drama. Thinking that it could be Lance, Sasha did not get up to answer the phone. Not even two minutes went by when her phone began to ring again. She hurried to answer it to prevent Tia from being woken up. She was surprised to see that it was Stacey; she was not in the mood to argue.

"Hey Stacey," Sasha answered in a melancholy tone.

"Hello to you, Sasha. I know that you're probably mad at me, but I love you anyway."

"Whatever," replied Sasha.

"Did you start your new job today?"

"Yes, I did, as well as found a babysitter for Tia."

"That's great. Who will be watching Tia for you?"

"Are you serious? Why do you care?"

"I care because she's my niece."

"You don't care. You're just nosey."

"That's not true. I do care. So who's keeping her?" Stacey asked.

"This lady a friend referred me to."

"A lady that a friend referred you to? So you don't know her?"

"Ugh. My friend knows her. This woman has watched kids for over twenty years"

"But Sasha, come on now. You don't have the best choice in friends. I'd be concerned about anyone who they might know or recommend."

"Well, for someone who isn't paying for my childcare, you have an awful lot to say. I'm not interested in your opinion right now," Sasha replied, even more annoyed than before.

"Girl, you'll leave that baby with people that you wouldn't even trust to hold your purse."

"Are you finished? That isn't true and I'm done with your interrogation. Tia is my daughter, not yours. When you decide to have kids, then you can do whatever you want. Oh, never mind, you're too selfish to have kids."

"You're right. It's your life. Just don't call me to fix your mistakes anymore."

"If you really cared, you would have helped me with my

childcare."

"Helped you? You mean enabled you. I just want you to grow up and to start making better choices."

"I'm trying to change," Sasha replied sincerely.

"I believe you. Well, enough of that. How did your first day go?"

"It went well. I think I'm going to like it. I might end up there permanently."

"You mean to tell me this is a temp job?"

"For now. But a lot of people are getting hired on directly."

"But Sasha, those people probably have a college degree and you don't."

"I have more than that. I have my looks and then some," Sasha stated.

"More than that? Sasha, you disgust me. You'll say anything to upset me, won't you?"

"I'm not worried about upsetting you. And I wasn't playing. My supervisor is already interested in me and he is *fine*. Trust me, he'll keep me around."

"That is so unprofessional. You should know better," Stacey said disapprovingly.

"I do know better."

"Momma didn't raise you like this. You should be ashamed of yourself. What happened to the attorney you were seeing?"

Sasha knew that this question was going to come up sooner or later. She was terribly embarrassed, although she tried to convince herself otherwise.

"Stacey, I wish I could go into all that right now, but I just don't have the energy. Trust me; you'll be glad that I left him alone."

"Maybe so, but you jump from man to man to man, and that's a hot mess. I don't want my niece around all those men," Stacey exclaimed.

"As much as I'd like to sit here and have you critique my life, I have better things to do. Call me tomorrow. Better yet, I'll call you," Sasha replied as she hung up on another sister.

## Chapter Eleven

Sasha sipped her coffee as she pulled into the parking lot of her new job. She was anxious to see Seth again and made sure that she wore one of her classiest dresses. Although she was excited to have arrived at work, her mind was occupied with Tia's lingering cries. Miss Susie seemed not to mind her temper tantrums, but Sasha hated to see her baby girl cry. She wanted to call to check on Tia but got distracted as she noticed Seth pulling up to the building. Her stomach started to flutter. She sipped her coffee one last time and intentionally left her phone in the car as she got out. Lance had blown up her phone all morning and she did not want to risk an interruption at work. It was obvious that he had a new phone and wanted to explain himself. *I should have known that destroying his phone wasn't going to stop the calls,* Sasha thought to herself as she licked the lipstick from her teeth.

Upon entering the building, Sasha realized that none of the new hires were in the orientation room. Confused and not knowing where to go, she went to the receptionist's desk.

"Good morning," the receptionist greeted her.

"Hello, and good morning to you. Would you please tell me where the orientation is being held today? I didn't see anyone in the room that we were in yesterday," Sasha said.

"Sure, one moment please," the receptionist instructed. Her

words were cordial, but her attitude was extremely cool.

"Seth will be training you today. He's on his way."

"Ok, thanks," Sasha replied.

She waited for several minutes. Then suddenly, she noticed Seth walking towards her with a confident swagger. He had a grin on his face that welcomed her and his cologne reached Sasha before he did.

"Good morning, Sasha. Follow me this way," Seth instructed. Sasha walked away with him happily. As they walked down the narrow hallway, Sasha brushed up against him intentionally several times, but he ignored her flirtatious behavior. Just as they were about to enter another room, he paused and handed Sasha his number.

"I want to get to know you, Sasha. You seem like a cool woman."

"You'd like to see me or get to know me? Please clarify," Sasha asked.

"I'd like to know you, but I don't want all these nosey people to be all in my business."

"Say no more," Sasha said in agreement.

"Ok, good. Well, let's get you trained," Seth stated as he watched Sasha walk past him into the room where several other

**Sasha**                                    **Marita Kinney**

people were gathered.

The work day was finally over and Sasha was thrilled to walk into her warm vanilla- scented apartment. Tia had cried herself to sleep and Sasha could not have been more relieved. Sasha hated whenever Tia became fussy for no apparent reason. Thankful that the babysitter fed Tia before she picked her up, therefore she wasn't crying due to hunger. Sasha became frustrated from brainstorming Tia's recent clingy behavior. She laid her down in her crib and hoped that she was out for the night. Sasha had no plans for the evening other than relaxing in a hot bubble bath while she listened to the radio. As she grabbed her towel from the back of her bedroom door, she thought about Seth and how sweet he seemed to be. There was something different about him and their attraction was strong. There was no indication of how things would go between them, but Sasha was willing to take the risk. She had marriage on her mind and Tia needed a father. Thinking of all the possibilities, she picked up her phone and sent him a quick text message to put the ball in his court.

"Hello, handsome, it's Sasha. I look forward to hearing from you," she typed quickly.

Instead of waiting for a reply, Sasha continued to the bathroom. As she ran water in the tub and poured the lavender bath salts into it, she began to daydream and ponder what Stacey told her about hopping from man to man. Although she hated getting unsolicited advice, she knew that there was some truth to Stacey's remarks. No one ever told her how to do things differently, but easily pointed out her mistakes. Stacey and Randi were the closest women to her and she respected their points of view. Texting Seth probably was not the best idea, but she was lonely. All she could think about was her sisters lying next to their husbands every night. The bath water was steaming hot as she gently placed each foot into the water. Lowering herself slowly into the tub, she began to think about her life in reality for the first time.

A couple of hours had passed and Sasha was still in the bathtub. Realizing that she had fallen asleep, she jumped out of the tub and wrapped herself in her towel. She tiptoed towards Tia's room, making a trail of wet footprints on the carpet. Tia was still sound asleep. After closing the door to Tia's room, she began to dry herself off as she walked back down the hallway to her room. Shocked that her cell phone was blinking, she dashed to see if Seth had texted her back. Unlocking the screensaver, Sasha smiled when she noticed that Seth had responded several times. Without hesitation, she replied quickly.

The two of them continued to text all night, until they could text no more. Sasha knew that she had made a terrible decision when she invited Seth over to keep her company. She wanted him badly, but did not want to lose her self-respect once again. Time was running out and he was on his way. Sasha went back and forth playing out different scenarios in her head. Although she wanted to un-invite him, she continued to apply scented lotions and perfume

**Sasha**                                    **Marita Kinney**

to prepare her body for a sexual encounter. Not having the courage to deny him, she walked towards the door when she heard a soft tap. She looked through the peephole and it was Seth. He was wearing a baseball cap and a sweat suit. Sasha was extremely attracted to him in his professional attire, but did not realize that he would be even more appealing to her in a baseball cap. Against her better judgment, she opened the door and greeted him with a passionate kiss. He was wearing the cologne that she loved and there was no turning back.

## Chapter Twelve

### One Month Later

The sun was shining brightly and Stacey could not wait to go to church. She had had a black eye for over a week and had been held hostage by her disfigurement. Larry's temper had gotten out of control once again. Stacey imagined how life would be if she had a marriage like Randi's and Russell's. She was considered to be the smart sister, but if everyone knew how badly Larry treated her, they would see how foolish she truly was. Stacey hated her life, but worked very hard to please Larry. It seemed like the more money she made, the happier Larry was. Her self-esteem was low and Larry would often remind her how he had rescued her from the hood. He took credit for all of her accomplishments and blamed her for any failure. Her sisters had no idea how she and Larry really lived. Larry isolated Stacey and she had not seen her sisters in over a month. Normally, they would have called her, but she understood that Randi was busy losing weight and committed to change, while Sasha, on the other hand, had started a new job and was occupied with a new love interest.

Stacey left the house without Larry and hoped that she could find a seat at church next to one of her sisters. She had convinced him that she needed to arrive a little early to help Randi with a women's group. She made sure that she applied enough makeup to hide any signs of abuse. Her business had not made any profit and Larry had taken it out on her. She needed some encouragement and needed her soul to be uplifted. Stacey tried to fight back the tears as she drove into the church parking lot. Shifting the gear into park, Stacey hopped out of the car and nearly ran inside. She could hear the choir from the parking lot, which instantly put her in a better mood. As she approached the main entrance to the church, the greeters welcomed her with a smile as they held the door open. She dreaded to see the tenant who owed her money. Church and money had always made her feel uncomfortable. She was not the one who liked to track down people for her money; however, the tenant had no idea how miserable things were for her at home because of the woman's past due balance. With the eviction papers in her purse, she was determined to confront the tenant after church.

Once inside the church, Stacey walked fast and eagerly to the sanctuary. She spotted Randi right away and asked the ushers to seat her there. Randi looked surprised to see Stacey sit down next to her. As Stacey took her seat, she hugged Randi and smiled at her nephews.

"Hey girl, where's Russell?" Stacey whispered.

"I'll tell you later. Where's Larry?" Randi echoed.

*On his way to Hell*, Stacey thought, then she laughed to herself just as she was about to reply.

"I guess he's still at home," Stacey whispered as she tried to hide her true feelings. The truth was that she really could care less where he was.

The two of them stopped their conversation and began to worship. Stacey looked over at Randi and began to cry. She admired her. Randi had actually changed a lot since the last time she had seen her. She was confident and glowing. Stacey was good at masking her feelings, but the Spirit of God was breaking her down. She was vulnerable. She was allowing herself to be purged. Randi glanced at Stacey and noticed how weak she appeared to be, so she grabbed both of her hands and began to pray with her as they both stood up from their pew. Stacey began to feel a shift in her spirit. The weight of the world was being lifted off of her. She began to feel hopeful instead of helpless. As they took their seats, an usher walked over and handed Stacey some tissue. She began to scan the congregation to see if Larry had arrived at church, but there was no sign of him anywhere. She was not surprised.

The pastor began to ask for a sacrificial offering. Stacey was never in favor of such an offering. She hated when people were begged to give. Randi looked at Stacey.

"What? Don't look at me, sis. I'm not paying for God to bless me," Stacey stated baldly.

Randi did not reply. They sat and watched as people walked towards the center aisle to give. Stacey's mouth literally fell open once the pastor asked for a two thousand dollar seed to be sown for the youth ministry.

"Stacey, stop looking like that. The money is for our youth," Randi exclaimed.

"It's not that. I can't believe what I'm seeing."

"What?" Randi asked, desperate to know what Stacey was referring to.

"That heifer just got in line."

"What? Who?" Randi asked, even more curious.

"My tenant, who is now three months behind. She must not have seen me come in, because she's not crazy. How is she going to sow anything? That's my money," Stacey said. "If she knew that I was here, she wouldn't have dared to stand up to give an offering. She's been dodging me for weeks.

"Oh no! Stacey, don't worry about it…"

Before Randi could finish her sentence, Stacey had grabbed her purse and walked towards the center aisle holding a piece of paper. As she approached the tenant, her rage blossomed. She walked up to the tenant and handed her the paper. The woman looked confused.

"You've just been evicted. Now get out of my house," Stacey demanded. The tenant did not reply, but just stood, shocked, in front of the whole congregation.

Stacey walked out of the church in a rage. Randi instantly got up to follow her. Seeing all of the commotion, the usher sat next to Randi's children.

"Stacey, wait!" Randi cried out as she continued to run behind her. Stacey finally began to slow down. As she approached her car, Randi could see that she was in tears.

"What's wrong, Stacey? What's going on?" Randi asked as she got into the passenger seat, refusing to allow Stacey to leave.

"I hate it when people take my kindness for weakness. My husband is breathing down my neck over that money and that heifer stood up there trying to sow something that she doesn't have to give. That's why I can't stand church people!" Stacey sobbed.

"This is all over money?" Randi asked.

"Boo, it's always over money," Stacey replied.

Randi gave Stacey a peculiar look, as if she wasn't quite sure what Stacey was referring to exactly. Before Stacey could reply, there was a tap on her back window.

"Sasha!" Randi blurted out.

Stacey unlocked the door to let her in.

"What are ya'll doing in here?" Sasha laughed as she hopped into the back seat.

"Girl, where did you come from? I didn't see you in the church," Randi asked.

"Don't worry about where I was," Sasha teased. "I'd like to know what transpired in there with Stacey. I've never seen her get so hood."

"Shut up, Sasha. That woman had the nerve to give the church two thousand dollars and she owes me almost three months' rent. Larry has been giving me hell over money lately. I just blew up. I don't know what happened."

"Girl, you've just lost the victory," Sasha said as she laughed to the point of tears. Stacey and Randi joined in.

"When was the last time that we laughed like this?"

"Randi, would you stop analyzing and being so deep all the time."

"Whatever, Sasha. Someone needs to have some logic and sense, because we all know that you don't have any," Randi replied.

"Well, look at you 'Miss Timid'. You've come out of your shell ever since that makeover, huh?" Stacey joked.

"About that. Stacey, I saw you leave the church and noticed some woman behind you. I thought to myself, who is the broad chasing after my sister. I was about to take off my earrings, then I saw the kids sitting with the usher and realized that it was Randi.

Girl, you look good!"

"Thank you so much, Sasha. That means a lot. Actually, that's why Russell isn't here today."

"Why is that?" asked Stacey.

"He's been tripping ever since you bought me those clothes. And oh my goodness, he can't stand the fact that I'm beginning to lose some weight."

"What? Russell's jealous?" Sasha laughed.

"Stop laughing, Sasha," Randi said. "He's really upset. I wasn't motivated to lose weight before. But after you messed with that married man I had to do something. Girl, you had me paranoid after that."

"Wait! What?" Stacey said, confused.

"See, Randi. Look what you've started," Sasha exclaimed. "Ok, Stacey, calm down. That attorney who you liked so much ended up being married. Randi came by right after I found out and I made her promise not to tell you. I was really embarrassed."

"You weren't that embarrassed. Didn't you tell me that you were seeing someone at your new job?" Stacey pointed out. Randi looked disgusted. She nodded her head and covered her ears to filter out any unwanted information.

"Yes, I did tell you that Stacey. However, this time it's

different."

Stacey and Randi began to laugh hysterically.

"Really, you guys. I think I love him," Sasha said.

"Love? Sasha, this guy hasn't even been with you through two menstrual cycles. What do you mean that you love him?" Randi asked in her motherly tone.

"He accepts me for being me. He's interested in Tia and makes us a priority. He adores Tia. I'm so blessed to have him in our lives. He puts her to bed at night and whenever she wakes up in the middle of the night, we take turns. I've always dreamed about having a father for her. Seth sometimes takes her to daycare for me, too. He's such a good man." Sasha blushed from raving about Seth to her sisters. She knew that they would be skeptical about her new love interest, so it was imperative that they hear only good things about him.

"I see that this man has you blushing awfully hard. What's his name?" Stacey asked.

"Seth. So can we change the subject?" Sasha suggested eagerly.

Randi laughed at how uncomfortable Sasha had become.

"Well, how's everything going with Tia's childcare?" Randi asked.

**Sasha**                                      **Marita Kinney**

Sasha rolled her eyes because she did not favor the topic that Randi chose to discuss.

"I found an affordable babysitter."

"Do you like her?"

"Why, Randi? Are you going to find me someone else? Are you offering to pay?" Sasha became irritated.

"I was simply asking, 'Miss Feisty'. No need to forget that you just got out of church."

"No, you're just being nosey. To answer your question, she's ok. She's older and seems to know what she's doing. But she always gets an attitude when I pick up Tia."

"Why? What did you do or not do?" Stacey jumped in and accused her.

Sasha began to laugh.

"See, I knew that you must have done something wrong." Stacey shook her head as Sasha confirmed her faults.

"Ok, Ok, I don't like her because she gets mad for me being on the phone when I pick up Tia."

"That's because you're being rude to that lady. She sat and watched your baby all day and you couldn't give her enough respect to get off the phone. Who are you usually talking to anyway?" Randi asked, disappointed yet again.

"I'm usually talking to Seth."

"Well, where is this Seth? Because we need to meet him right away," Stacey insisted.

"He's still inside the church with Tia."

"What? That's impressive…Oh my goodness, I forgot that my kids are still inside too." Randi threw open the car door and ran back inside. Sasha got out of the car and followed behind her.

"I'll call you guys later," Stacey yelled from her car window as she drove off.

## Chapter Thirteen

"Hello, Randi."

"Good afternoon, Sasha. How are you?"

Sasha pulled up to her apartment but did not turn off the car. She sighed as she glanced back at Tia.

"I'm good. I just don't understand why Tia cries so much."

"She's a baby, Sasha. What do you expect her to do?"

"I know that she may whine at times, but not like this. She cries and screams every morning when I drop her off at the babysitter. Then it's the same thing when I pick her up."

"Have you considered that Tia may not like her babysitter?"

"Of course, but I don't have any other choice. I can't afford to take her anywhere else."

"What is she doing now?" Randi asked.

"She cried herself to sleep again. Sometimes she'll stay asleep all night and won't even get up to eat dinner."

"What? Something isn't right about that," Randi said. "You've been taking her there for over six months."

"Exactly. Seth said that I should look into a childcare

**Sasha**                          **Marita Kinney**

center and that he'd pay half. Randi, you already know how I am. I'm not about to rely on no man. Then if he gets mad and decides to leave, I'm stuck with the bill. No ma'am, I don't think so."

"How is that going anyway?"

"What? Seth and me?" she confirmed as she turned up the heat to make herself more comfortable. It was extremely cold outside and she didn't feel like carrying Tia inside just yet.

"Yes! You and Mr. Seth."

"We're good! I'm just not used to a man around me all the time. He comes over for dinner and stays over nearly every night to be exact."

"Sasha, it sounds like you're playing house."

"No, I'm not. We just spend a lot of time together. Randi, he really wants to be in my life. It's getting pretty serious between us. I think he may ask me to marry him soon."

"Wow. I wasn't expecting that."

"I know. I wasn't either. He's been bringing it up lately though. But we'll see what happens. I need to have a ring placed on my finger first. I don't want to jump to any premature conclusions."

"I'm happy for you. I hope everything works out. God honors marriage. I've always wanted to see you walk down the aisle."

"See! Now you're jumping to conclusions," Sasha giggled.

"OK, OK, OK," Randi laughed. "Well, I have to go. Russell just walked through the door."

"Ok, I love you," Sasha said.

"I love you too, baby sis."

Sasha hung up the phone feeling happy and less frustrated. Randi had a way of making her feel better.

## Chapter Fourteen

"Baby, I'm going to call you back. I think Tia is finally getting up."

"Alright love! Don't worry about calling me back tonight. I'll just see you tomorrow."

"I miss you. I can't wait until tomorrow," Sasha murmured.

"I miss you too, baby. I wanted to come over there tonight, but I had to do laundry."

"I could have done it for you."

"I know, baby! But I wouldn't do that to you. You have enough on your plate. Just call me when you wake up in the morning."

"Sure thing. I love you, Seth."

"I love you too, Sasha."

She pulled back her comforter and hurried to get Tia.

"Hey honey! Are you hungry?"

Tia simply laid her head on Sasha's shoulder and wrapped her legs around her waist. The night shirt that Sasha was wearing started to get wet from Tia's diaper. She realized that she had not changed her since she got home. Sasha got the diaper bag and laid

**Sasha**                                    **Marita Kinney**

Tia on the floor in front of her. As she began to unbutton Tia's
onesie, she noticed how Tia began to squirm around. Frustrated
and not in the mood to play, Sasha commanded Tia to lie still. She
finally had restrained her enough to open her diaper. What she saw
overwhelmed her and she began to gasp for air. She closed her
eyes and picked up her sweet baby. But the sight of the blood that
stained Tia's diaper was burned into her brain. "Oh Lord," she
cried out, feeling nauseated and bewildered. Her head started to
spin out of control with awful thoughts. She wanted to believe that
the blood was caused by a urinary tract infection. The more she
tried to justify the blood-stained diaper, the more she felt that
something terrible had occurred. Sasha bit her lip and tried to
control her rage. Unable to restrain herself, she began to throw and
break anything that she could grab. "NO GOD, NO," Sasha
pleaded as she covered up Tia's innocent pearl with a wet wipe.
Her heart felt like it was about to leap out of her chest; she felt
helpless. She uncovered Tia to exam her more thoroughly.
Instantly she recognized that her flower was raw and red—nothing
like a diaper rash or anything she had ever seen before. She knew
without a doubt that her baby girl had been molested. Her strange
behavior started to make sense. "Tia, you don't play with a baby
doll like that. Where did you learn this from?" Sasha remembered
the time she noticed Tia trying to insert her fingers between the
baby doll's legs. The thought made her want to vomit. The tears of
pain trickled slowly down her cheeks as she tried to smile and stay
strong for her baby, who lay confused and uncertain.

**Sasha**                                    **Marita Kinney**

Feeling faint, she tried calling the babysitter, but was unable to dial her number. Her hands were shaking uncontrollably. Desperate to question and confront Miss Susie, Sasha took her frustration out on her phone. Throwing it against the wall, she watched it break into tiny pieces. Tia still lay there, quietly and innocently, while Sasha continued to torment herself. She could not believe that she had kept taking Tia to Miss Susie's. It was clear that Tia did not want to go over there, but she continued to take her anyway; Sasha began to feel guilty that she was too interested in Seth to worry about Tia and what Tia was trying to tell her.

With no way to call anyone for help, she buttoned up Tia's clothes and stormed out of the house. As she strapped Tia into her car seat, tears fell and her vision blurred. Slamming the car door shut, she realized that she did not know where she was going. The air was freezing and the steam from her breath blew out like a bull. She got into the car and flew off. All she could think about was revenge. Her pain overcame her as if she was having a terrible nightmare but could not wake up. Snot ran down to her lip. She tried to wipe it away with the back of her hand. A million thoughts ran through her mind, but none of them were of God. She desperately needed something to calm her nerves. God seemed not to hear her cries, so alcohol became her solution. She remembered suddenly that she had an unopened bottle of vodka in the trunk of her car. Drinks at the club were always so expensive that she kept her own bottle with her. It became a routine for Sasha and her girl friends to get drunk right before they started partying.

There was a nearby gas station and Sasha needed somewhere to park. As she pulled into the lot, she thought about what she was going to do. She knew that she had to do something to protect Tia, but her options seemed few. "Pop." Sasha opened up her trunk. She smiled as soon as she saw her comfort drink. Quickly she sat back in the front seat and opened the bottle. Vodka dripped down her chin as she downed the burning alcohol. It felt like fire as it went down her throat, but it could not compare to the pain that she felt in her heart. Minutes went by and she still did not feel a buzz. Trying to avoid drawing attention to herself, she rushed to put the empty bottle back inside the trunk. She opened the trunk again and threw the bottle in. As the trunk door was closing, Sasha spotted her empty gas container. Seth had put it in her trunk for emergencies, just in case she ever ran out of gas. Sasha could not ignore her feelings of rage. She began to stare at the red container. Instead of putting aside her thoughts, she chose to entertain them. A deviant grin came over Sasha's face. Tia began to cry. *She's probably hungry*, Sasha thought. The more Tia cried, the more Sasha's mood deteriorated. The gas station's pumps became more and more appealing to her evil thoughts. She drove swiftly to the closest pump. Looking at Tia through the back window, Sasha began to fill up the empty container and gas started to spill over the sides. She began to feel the effects of the vodka.

**Sasha**                                    **Marita Kinney**

She put the heavy gas-filled container in the passenger side seat, spilling gas everywhere; the station attendant peeked out of the door to see if she needed help. He yelled, "You got it?" Sasha did not reply. She drove off leaving her credit card still in the slot at the pump.

Drunk and determined to prove a point, Sasha drove up to Miss Susie's house. It was dark and the neighborhood was quiet. She grabbed the container of gas and closed the car door with her foot. She could hear Tia's cries from outside the car. She closed her eyes and paused. Then, proceeding towards Miss Susie's house, she began to pour gas around the perimeter. Not satisfied, she then walked up on the porch to pour out the last few drips that remained. Just as she tried to retrieve the lighter that she often carried with her, she looked down and saw one laying on the porch as if the devil himself had placed it there. Extremely drunk and more relaxed, she fumbled to light it. On her third try, just as she began to walk away, the lighter finally caught. She tossed it on the porch and the flames flickered in her blood-shot eyes like powerful demons.

## Chapter Fifteen

"What's wrong? Who was that on the phone?"

"Not now, Larry." Stacey dropped the cell phone, jumped out of bed, and began to throw on anything that she could find.

"What are you doing, Stacey?"

"That was the police station. They have Tia."

"Huh?"

"They said that if I didn't come down there to get her, protective services would send her to foster care," Stacey cried.

"Where's Sasha?"

"I DON'T KNOW. I DON'T KNOW ANYTHING. I have to go. I'll call you as soon as I know something," Stacey yelled as she rushed out the door. On her way to the car she began to call Sasha's cell phone. Nothing. It went straight to voice mail.

"RING, RING, RING." Stacey waited impatiently for Randi to pick up. As she located the police station's address in her navigation system, Randi finally answered.

"Hel...lo."

"Randi! Wake up."

"Stacey, what's up? Why are you calling so late?"

"I'm on my way to the police station to get Tia. The police just called me."

"Going *where*? To get *who*?" Randi sat up in bed to make sure that she had heard Stacey correctly.

"Have you heard from Sasha?" Stacey asked anxiously.

"Earlier. I spoke to her when she got off work. What's going on?"

"I have no idea. The police just called me and said that I need to come pick Tia up," Stacey replied in a panic.

"Oh my goodness. Ok, I'll meet you there. I'm on my way." Randi slammed down the phone.

Stacey was beyond worried. Clueless about the situation, she rushed to get Tia. The thought of her going to foster care was horrifying. The speedometer said eighty-five miles per hour and it was not nearly as fast as Stacey desired.

"Turn left," instructed the navigation system. Stacey pumped her brakes to slow down. She spotted the police station and began to wipe her tears as she parked. Goose bumps covered her body as the midnight wind blew across her silk pajama top. She realized suddenly that she had forgotten to grab her coat. The station appeared to be quiet, and it was not at all like she had expected. She walked up to the clerk's desk.

"May I help you?"

"Yes. Someone called me about thirty minutes ago to pick up my niece. Her name is Tia Watson."

"Oh, ok. You're here to pick up the baby?"

"Yes, ma'am," Stacey replied, her voice trembling.

"Do you know where my sister Sasha is?"

"Have a seat and someone will be right with you," the clerk said as if she was used to people picking up babies from jail in the middle of the night.

Stacey had sat for almost twenty minutes when the door flew open. It was Randi.

"Randi!" Stacey shouted.

Randi walked over to Stacey and gave her a huge, heartfelt hug.

"Where's Tia and Sasha?"

"I don't know yet. They just told me to have a seat."

Randi sighed and sat next to Stacey. Several minutes later a tall, slender man in a police uniform walked towards them.

"Hello, I'm Officer White. Thank you for coming down here under these circumstances.

"That's why we're confused. We have no idea what's going on. Someone called me and told me to come pick up my niece," Stacey explained.

"Yes, ma'am. I called you. I'm afraid something terrible has happened tonight."

Randi and Stacey braced themselves to hear the news.

"Who is Sasha in relation to you?" asked the officer.

"She's our sister," Stacey and Randi replied in unison.

"There was a fire tonight—arson. We have reason to believe that your sister started it. Two people were killed."

"WHAT? What makes you think that?" Randi blurted out.

"We found her at the scene of the accident. We also found who appeared to be her daughter in the back seat of her car, which was left running and unattended."

"Which one of you ladies is Stacey?"

"I'm Stacey," she announced as she massaged her temple to relieve her headache.

"We contacted you because you were listed on her registration," stated the officer.

"Oh, Lord," Stacey shouted. "Is she ok? Where's Tia? Where's Sasha?"

"The baby is with one of our social workers at St. Rita's hospital. We took her there to make sure that she wasn't injured. Unfortunately, during her exam they discovered that she has been sexually abused. We can't share all the details with you at this time, but we have reason to believe that your sister went to Susie Anderson's house to confront her."

"WHAT," Randi shouted in disbelief.

"I wanted to speak to you before I released the baby into your care. However, your sister, on the other hand, is unconscious and in critical care. She has suffered third degree burns and has been taken to the hospital as well." Randi buried her face in her hands and started to weep, while Stacey frowned intensely to fight back her own tears.

"Can we see Sasha?" Randi asked.

"I'm afraid not at this time. She's in police custody. The sheriff will have to approve your visit."

"You're telling us that our sister has been severely burned and that our niece was molested. What do you mean that we can't go see her until the sheriff gives us approval?" Stacey asked.

"As I said, I can't go into all the details. But two people lost their lives tonight and your sister did it." They were momentarily speechless and then Stacey found her voice.

"WHAT? What makes you think that she tried to kill them? Sasha would never do anything so terrible," she insisted.

"Sasha told me that Tia would cry nonstop every time she dropped her off. She felt that something could be wrong. I shouldn't have gotten off the phone with her," Randi said regretfully.

"I can't believe this. This has to be a nightmare," Stacey exclaimed.

"If you have any additional information, you can call me anytime. We're working diligently on this case. Due to your sister's condition, you'll probably be allowed to see her in the next few days." The officer looked at them compassionately. "Whenever you're ready, you can pick up your niece."

"How is she?" Randi asked.

"Scared. She's extremely scared. A lot has happened tonight," the officer replied.

"I can't believe this," Randi repeated.

"Yes, I'll let the social worker know that you're on your way. She'll need to ask you a series of questions before Tia is released. Don't worry, it shouldn't take long."

Stacey and Randi were speechless. Their family had been turned upside down.

## Chapter Sixteen

"Honey, please turn that TV off. I don't want to watch those people make my little sister out to be some kind of monster."

"This is crazy. They're trying to charge Sasha with two counts of aggravated murder, arson, and child endangerment. They're talking about her as if they don't care that she got burned too. When will you be allowed to see your Sasha?"

"I have no idea. I guess we're supposed to just sit around and wait until the Sheriff or some heartless person decides to approve our visit. They said that she's in critical care. My sister could be dying," Stacey cried.

"I'm sorry that your family is going through all this."

"The news is not reporting facts. They're just speculating. Sasha is in intensive care and no one knows the whole story," Stacey argued with the television.

"Stacey, you have to admit that Sasha could have very well killed those people. She has some anger issues," added Larry.

"You don't want to go there with me. You've been hitting me for years and you want to talk about anger issues," Stacey stated, rolling her eyes at him.

"Whatever, Stacey. You make me upset sometimes. But I didn't kill anyone."

"You're so insensitive, Stacey commented under her breath.

To avoid even more tension, she went upstairs to the spare bedroom and lay next to Tia. She began to play various scenarios in her head, but nothing seemed to make much sense. The police would not release much information about the case. The unknown haunted her and she desperately needed some answers.

Stacey rolled over to get comfortable and noticed that the bed was soaked with urine. She realized that she had not changed Tia's diaper, that her mind was preoccupied with the tragic situation. She tiptoed over to the diaper bag that the social worker gave her, which was not Tia's original bag. The mere fact that Tia was given some cheap plastic bag was a reminder that things were different. Sasha would never have carried such a bag. Stacey began to cry as she reminisced how Sasha begged her to buy such an expensive diaper bag. Stacey began to change Tia. As she took off her soiled diaper, Tia cried and resisted. She kicked her legs and screamed uncontrollably. Stacey was livid. Tia showed clear signs that she had indeed been molested. Tears flooded Stacey's eyes. She could no longer be in denial about what had occurred. She could only imagine the hurt that Sasha felt as Tia's mother. Stacey then knew without a doubt that Sasha intended to kill whoever had hurt her baby.

# Chapter Seventeen

After several days of waiting, Stacey and Randi were finally allowed to see Sasha. The waiting room was quiet and the air was dry.

"I hate hospitals," Stacey complained, annoyed by the long wait. Randi remained silent and just listened to Stacey's long list of complaints.

"How's everything going with Tia?" Randi asked to change the subject.

"She's good. It's so different having her at our house. It's been good for me to take this time off, but Larry and I have a lot of work to catch up on. I'm glad that I have the flexibility to be with Tia right now. When are you coming to get her?" Stacey asked. "Because I can't believe that Larry is at home with her."

"Stacey, I can maybe help with her a couple days a week. But I'm in no position to take on another child. Russell and I are barely making it with our four boys."

"So what are you suggesting, Randi? I can't keep Tia permanently. Who knows how long all this is going to last."

"I'll help you any way that I can. I just can't have her live with us. Russell and I are really struggling financially right now."

"Randi, do not pull the money card on me."

"It takes money to raise a child and I already have a house full of kids. You and Larry do not. Stop being selfish, Stacey. This is for our sister," Randi stated before she was interrupted by a nurse.

"Thank you for your patience. Please follow me. Before you go into the room, please keep in mind that she has had several surgeries and is extremely weak. It takes a lot of strength to speak, so please don't ask her any questions. I must warn you that about sixty percent of her body has third degree burns," the young nurse advised. "Also, I apologize, but she cannot have any flowers. She is highly prone to infection right now."

Randi collapsed on the floor and Stacey knelt down and began to rub her back to comfort her.

The nurse took a deep breath. "If you two need a few minutes to prepare yourselves, please take your time."

"No. We'll go now," Randi said, with a boldness and strength she did not really feel as she picked herself up off the floor.

Stacey and Randi held hands as they prepared to enter Sasha's hospital room. As the door opened, they were greeted by two police officers who began to pat them down. Another nurse sat next to Sasha's bed.

"You have twenty minutes," one of the officers announced. Randi and Stacey could not reply. There were so many tubes and

## Sasha                        Marita Kinney

Sasha was unrecognizable. Her bandages covered her whole body. She resembled a mummy.

"Sasha, Boo. It's us...Stacey and Randi." There was no response.

"Don't worry about anything, Tia is with me," Stacey said as her voice began to crack.

"Honey, she hears you, look," the nurse said and pointed. Stacey and Randi both looked at Sasha and noticed a tear forming in the corner of her right eye. They stood in amazement.

Randi pulled a small bottle of oil from her pocket. As she unscrewed the top, an officer approached her.

"What do you think you're doing?" he asked. "I'm about to anoint my sister." The officer looked confused. "She's entitled to her religious customs, correct?" Randi asked as she continued to pour the oil onto her index fingers.

"Yes, she is," the officer replied when he realized that they were preparing to have prayer. Randi began to anoint the bed post, starting from the foot board all the way up to the headboard, where she gently applied a cross. Speaking in another tongue, she took the bottle of oil and dripped one drop onto Sasha's forehead. Stacey watched and began to admire Randi's faith. Randi reached for Stacey's hand and they began to pray over their baby sister as she struggled for her life.

"Dear God, we come to you as humbly as we know how and ask that you step in and take control of every aspect of this situation. Lord God, we ask you for healing and restoration of Sasha and the other family that's been affected. As we understand that you are a God with unlimited power, we come to you and ask for mercy. God, we ask that your will be done and we believe in your power and seal this prayer in Jesus' Name, Amen."

"Amen," Stacey added.

Just as they were getting ready to exit the room, Stacey turned to look at Sasha one last time. The tear that once lay in the corner of her eye had found its way down her cheek. Randi and Sasha looked at each other and smiled. They held hands once again, and walked out of the room with their heads held high and their spirits lifted.

## Chapter Eighteen

"Can you pass me the sugar?" Randi asked as she tasted her coffee and realized that it was not sweet enough. Stacey reached for the sugar packets and placed them in front of Randi.

"It's going to be ok," Randi reassured her as she tore open the packets. Stacey's eyes began to fill with tears as she thought about Sasha. Randi began to share a funny childhood story to lighten the mood.

"Randi, I almost forgot how funny you are," Stacey laughed.

"What do you mean by that? I've always been the funniest sister."

"Yeah, until you started going to church and getting all deep," Stacey teased. The waitress began to place their food in front on them.

"This food looks so good. I haven't eaten like this since I went on my diet."

"Yes, it does look good," Stacey agreed. "Hey Randi, can you go ahead and bless the food? Larry keeps blowing up my phone and I need to call him back. He's probably calling to see how Sasha's doing. Don't wait on me, I'll be right back," Stacey said as she stood up and excused herself from the table. Randi bowed her head to bless the food, but was distracted by Stacey's conversation. Although she had walked towards the restroom, her voice could be heard from the table. Randi started on her food and did not want to pry. Several minutes later, Stacey rejoined her at the table. It was obvious that she was upset.

"Are you ok?" Stacey looked at Randi as if she wanted to reply. With a sarcastic smile, her body language spoke on her behalf.

"Stacey, what's wrong? Is Tia alright?" Randi inquired.

"Tia's fine," Stacey replied tersely.

"Well, something's wrong," Randi insisted.

"Larry asked me when you were going to pick up Tia," Stacey replied as she looked down at the table and sighed.

"Really? You only went to the hospital and he's ready to get rid of Tia already. Did you tell him that you're almost finished eating?"

"Randi, just stop it. It has nothing to do with me leaving Tia with him. He doesn't want her there…period," Stacey replied, embarrassed. She could not bring herself to see the disappointment on Randi's face.

"After all this time, I thought you were just selfish. Larry really doesn't like kids, does he? Stacey, answer me." Stacey stared out of the restaurant's window. "I can't believe that Larry is being so insensitive during such a time. There is no way that Russell and I can keep her. We don't have money for another child. Let's be honest. Once Sasha recovers, she'll be in jail until this whole thing is figured out and who knows how long that will be. We have to work together. Can't you make him see that?" Randi pleaded as she looked down at her plate, her appetite gone altogether.

"No, I can't convince him. Two years ago I became pregnant." Randi's eyes widened. "He began to treat me terribly. Randi, it was like he became a monster. He despised me and made sure that I knew it. He blamed the whole pregnancy on me. I told Larry that God didn't make mistakes. He agreed. Then he said maybe God doesn't, but I did because I allowed myself to get pregnant after he told me that he didn't want any children. I cried endlessly. He drove me to an abortion clinic and waited outside. After the procedure was over, he forced me to attend a fund raising meeting. I believe that Tia reminds him of what happened."

"Stacey, I had no idea. I'm sorry that you have to live like that," Randi mumbled as she tried to resist crying, but couldn't. She saw the pain in Stacey's eyes.

"I love my husband and I thought that we were on the same page. I never wanted children until I became pregnant. My baby would have been the same age as Tia. Sasha never understood why I gave her such a hard time. That's why. I hated to watch her being so irresponsible and I hated to see you as a great mother. I was torn and Larry didn't care. After my abortion, he made me agree to a tubal ligation. I wanted to keep my marriage together, so I went through with it. Due to my age, my doctor agreed to do it." Stacey dropped her head in shame.

"I can't believe this. Stacey, I'm so sorry. How could I not have noticed you hurting like that? I wish I'd known. I wish I could have been there for you. I care and we'll get through this. As soon as I get home, I'll try to talk to Russell. Maybe he'll reconsider keeping Tia. God will provide a way for us to take her."

"Randi, I can't allow you to do that."

"Huh? Why not?"

"Because I've just made up my mind. Tia is staying with me. God doesn't make mistakes. This is not only helping Sasha, but I believe that God has ordained this situation to heal me also." Randi got up, sat next to Stacey in the booth and hugged her. Stacey laid her head on Randi's shoulder and sobbed.

## Chapter Nineteen

### Eight months later

"This is so confusing. What do you mean that I can't plead insanity? Once I saw that blood in my baby's diaper I literally lost my mind. What's not insane about that?"

"Sasha, I understand your frustration. But they have proof that you went to a gas station and filled up an empty container. That's enough evidence to prove that everything was premeditated."

"What proof?"

"The attorney said that the prosecutor had your credit card in evidence. Apparently you left it at the station. They even have you on surveillance filling up the container." There was silence on the other end of the phone, and then sniffling echoed down the line.

"Sasha, I'm here for you."

"I know, Stacey. What's my baby doing?"

"She's taking a nap. She was so excited when I brought her to see you for her birthday."

"How could I ever forget? When she first saw me she was so scared. But then when she heard my voice, she instantly remembered that I was mommy. She began to look past my scars. It's as if she doesn't see what everyone else sees. God only shows her my love. She only sees mommy," Sasha cried.

"Sasha, you'll always be more beautiful than I am. God has been showing me so much about myself and nothing about me is pretty," Stacey replied.

"I'm thankful for you. Stacey, you *are* beautiful. You have just allowed hurt to control you. Tia will show you how beautiful you are. Kids have a way of doing that," Sasha laughed and then began to cry again. "I miss her so much."

"She misses you too. We all do."

"Did Seth ever contact you?" Sasha asked with anticipation.

"Sasha, please, just concentrate on your case."

"You haven't talked to him at all, have you?" Sasha asked as she started to come to the realization that Seth had moved on.

"Look, honey, let's just focus on your case and getting you better," Stacey suggested.

"My scars aren't going anywhere, Stacey. And I'm not getting out. Why do I continue to think that one day I'll wake up and all of this will have been a nightmare?" She began to weep.

**Sasha**                                          **Marita Kinney**

Before Stacey could reply, the call ended. She hated when the calls timed out and the last thing she heard was Sasha crying. She was desperate to fight for Sasha's freedom but was becoming worn out herself. The attorney's fees had drained her account. After Larry left, she would have nothing but her struggling business and her life's savings.

Stacey felt terrible and did not want to burden Sasha with her martial problems. It was only a matter of time before Larry would walk out of her life. She pretended not to see the divorce papers laying on the kitchen counter. It was the elephant in the room, but was also the least of her worries. Her little sister was going to spend the rest of her life in prison for murder and arson; divorce was the farthest thing from her mind. With no energy to fight for her marriage, she had decided to let it go.

"Was that Sasha on the phone?" Larry asked as he walked into the room bringing his attitude with him.

"Yes, dear." Stacey replied, trying to keep the conversation to a minimum. She knew that he had intended to argue with her, but she was not going to give in to his drama.

"So, did you tell her that she wasn't getting out anytime soon and that her baby is about to go to a foster home or somewhere?" Larry stared at Stacey, anticipating a response that was sure to get her smacked.

"Larry, thank you for everything. You've taught me a lot and I'll always be grateful for that. You've taught me how to believe in myself when no one else will, how to forgive people who hurt me, and most importantly, how to pray. Tia will not be going to a foster home. God put her in my care for a reason. She's my niece, not some puppy that you return. If you choose to leave me, that's fine. I've already seen the divorce papers on the counter," Sasha stated firmly and confidently.

"You're stupid, Stacey. You're going to let Sasha ruin your life. She killed those people. Why should we have to suffer too?"

"Suffer? Sasha may have committed a horrible crime, but she didn't ruin my life. We're guilty of murder too. Oh, but it's justified because it was called an abortion, right?" Larry walked towards Stacey with his eyes full of rage. Stacey did not flinch.

"What? You want to hit me, right?" Stacey asked boldly, her arms folded.

"Nope. I'm not going to touch you. So you think that I'm a murderer just like your trashy sister, huh?" Larry sat down on the bed and awaited a reply. Instead, Stacey began to cry.

"I wish that you would stop judging my sister. We're no better than she is."

"I'm not a killer. You are, sweetie. You killed our baby," Larry said sarcastically.

"You bastard. You made me get that abortion because you didn't want to have kids." Stacey's lower lip trembled.

"You're mistaken, dear. I just never wanted to have children with you. I already have two kids." Stacey's stomach dropped. "You never wondered why I travel so much or why I have college funds set aside? The accounts statements come here every month." Stacey gently placed her hand over her womb. "You're lying. Larry, tell me that you're lying." Instead of replying, Larry stood in his truth and watched with pleasure as Stacey's heart shattered into a million pieces. Hitting Stacey could not inflict the pain that her heart had just suffered.

## Chapter Twenty

"You look good, Randi. Oh my goodness, look at you." Stacey put her hands on her hips to exam Randi's new physique thoroughly. "I'm jealous. Look at your butt. What does Russell think about all of this?" Stacey asked as she hand motioned a coke bottle shape for Randi's figure.

"Thanks so much, Stacey. That means a lot coming from you. Russell is so insecure now. I honestly think that he'd rather me be overweight. I just don't understand him." Stacey listened with little compassion.

"Oh my goodness. He needs to stop tripping," Stacey replied as she sipped on her coffee.

"He gave me a hard time today because I was coming to meet you."

"Are you serious? Did you tell him that we were meeting about Sasha's case?"

"Girl, he doesn't care. He thinks that every man is looking at me," Randi laughed.

"Hon, I just don't know what you're going to do about that. Your sexy new look has Russell all paranoid. You're going to have to leave the house in rollers or a head scarf to make him feel comfortable." They both laughed.

"I could be wearing that and a jogging suit. If men have a desire to look, they will. It doesn't matter if I wear a skirt down to my ankles or I cover up like a Muslim. He just needs to know that I'm woman enough to be fly and still honor my husband." Stacey high-fived Randi.

"Exactly. Ok, Randi let's get started, because I have to hurry up and get you back home. Russell's not about to come looking for me," Stacey said jokingly. "No, but really, I'm not going to keep you long because I have to pick Tia up from daycare.

"How is Sasha?" Randi asked. "She hasn't called me in a few weeks."

"She's up and down. She misses Tia incredibly and of course her scars are bothering her. It takes a while for her to warm up, but she's still the feisty Sasha that we all know and love."

"Have you told her about Seth yet?"

"No. I couldn't bring myself to tell her. I asked the attorney to let me talk to her first. He didn't want me to, but I'm concerned what she may do. Her self-esteem is so low…" Stacey could not complete her sentence.

"I just pray that God gives her strength," Randi added.

"Yes, we all need that. I'm going to tell her the next time she calls."

Randi could tell that something else was bothering Stacey and decided to fish for more details.

"Now Stacey, you know that I'm not the type of person that tries to get all up in your business, but how are things going with you at home?"

"Home is home," Stacey said as she tried to avoid the real issue.

"So what does that mean? Does that mean that Larry is still crazy Larry?"

Stacey smirked. "That's exactly what that means. He wants a divorce and I just want peace. I can no longer live like that. It's not just me anymore; I have to think about Tia."

"Oh my goodness, Stacey. I'm so sorry."

"No, I'm sorry that I allowed him to change me. But through this tragedy with Sasha, I've somehow found myself again.

## Chapter Twenty-one

The phone rang just as Stacey was laying Tia in her twin canopy toddler bed. Her heart dropped, knowing that it was probably Sasha calling. She always tried to call around Tia's bedtime. Any other time, Stacey would be glad to hear from her, but not tonight. She looked at her caller ID. It was Sasha and butterflies filled her stomach as she answered the phone.

"Hello."

"You have a collect call from an inmate in the Western Valley Correctional Institute. Do you wish to accept this call?" the automated system asked. "Press '1' to accept."

"Beep..." Stacey held down the number '1' key as she hesitated to be connected.

"Hello?" Stacey answered, pretending to be calm.

"Hey, Stacey. Were you asleep?" Sasha asked, hearing the peculiar tone of Stacey's voice.

"Huh uh. But Tia is."

"Oh no, she is? I called as soon as I could," Sasha replied, instantly disappointed.

"Sasha, I met with your attorney the other day like you asked me to..."

"Oh! What did he say about my trial?" Sasha asked anxiously.

Stacey took a few seconds to reply. "What? Stacey. Why are you so quiet?

"I'm afraid that I have some bad news."

"Bad news? What kind of bad news?"

"The attorney was given some vital information. As I have power of attorney for you, he contacted me first. He'll give you all the details tomorrow morning."

"Stacey, what details? You're scaring me," Sasha gasped.

"They have CPS complaints against you."

"CPS complaints? Huh? What? CPS, what's that?" Sasha asked, irritated and confused.

"Child Protective Services," Stacey explained.

"WHAT? WHY? I wasn't always the best mother, but Stacey, you know that I would never hurt Tia."

"Yes. Yes, I know. Sasha, there's more."

"More?"

"Yes, more." Stacey rubbed her eyes as tears began to fall. "Miss Susie filed the complaints. Several times, actually."

"I can't believe this. Why would she do something like that? None of this makes any sense to me."

"She reported that Tia could possibly have been being molested by your boyfriend, Seth."

"Ah HUH, ah HUH, ah HUH! UHHHHHHHHHHH!" Sasha wept bitterly. "So I kil…." the words would not come out of her mouth as she continued to mourn.

"Yes. Miss Susie was trying to help Tia. The reports show that she was extremely concerned. The last time that she filed a complaint was on that day."

"Why didn't she say something to me?"

"Apparently she tried."

Sasha opened her eyes. Tears ran down her melted face and there wasn't a dry eye in the room. The female prisoners all looked at Sasha, giving her their respect.

## Chapter Twenty-two
## Seventeen Years Later

"I'm in here for life, but y'all have another chance to make different decisions," she told them. 'Vengeance is mine, saith the Lord'. I was a fool. I tried to get my own revenge, but instead I killed two innocent people who were trying to help me. Satan made me feel like I could take matters into my own hands. He lied. That's what he does best. He's a liar. Some people thought that my life was over. However, God showed me that it was just the beginning." Sasha smiled with pride and accomplishment. She looked sorrowfully at the inmates, "Are there any questions?"

"What happened to that guy, Seth?" an inmate asked.

"Good question. Once I got burned up and locked up, he vanished. He was nowhere to be found. Next question."

"Is your daughter Tia still with your sister Stacey?" another inmate asked.

"No. She's a freshman in college now, studying criminal justice. Are there any more questions?"

"Are you mad at God?" asked yet another inmate. The woman's face was beet red and tears streamed down her face. She tried to contain herself but she was overcome with emotion.

"No. I'm not angry with God. Being in here saved my life. Although I'm here in prison, I'm the freest that I've ever been. Outside these walls, I was a selfish burden on so many people. Now God has chosen me to help women like you."

"One more question," the correctional guard advised.

"What happened to your sisters?" an inmate asked from across the room.

"Stacey is doing extremely well with her company and has done an amazing job raising Tia. Tia taught her how to love and how to forgive. Her ex-husband Larry remarried and had three more kids. Stacey was bitter for years, but I believe that Tia was sent to her by God. My job was to give birth to her, but Stacey was supposed to raise her. As for Randi, well, she has become a physical trainer. Her husband was her first client. They now work together, training and educating people about their health. She claims that I motivated her to lose weight, so she named the company 'Sasha Fit'."

"What was the greatest lesson that you have learned?" asked the prison guard as she tried to maintain her composure.

"I learned to live. I learned to love myself, and I learned that everything that Satan had intended to kill me with, God turned it around and made it beautiful. I have a testimony. My testimony is someone else's hope.

## Conclusion

How many of us can identify with Sasha, Stacey, or Randi? It is amazing how God can take the tragedy of one person's life and use it to change the lives of others: Sasha was not only guilty of murder, she was guilty of chasing the idea of being with a man. She wanted him so badly that she missed the red flags along the way. There are some women today who still struggle with loneliness and become desperate to fill that void. That was the case with Sasha. Being controlled by her loneliness led her to destructive habits and actions. We all want to be loved, but look for it in the wrong places. God wants to fill that void. God wants to show you the agape love that he has for you. Anything other than God is temporary. Why do you think that so many women hop from man to man? It is simple; it is temporary; happiness is not money; happiness is not a marriage; happiness is not your appearance or social status. Happiness is loving the person God made you to be and loving *her* unconditionally. Sasha did not find happiness until she was sent to prison and for the first time in her life became truly free.

About the Author

# Who is Marita Kinney?

**Marita L Kinney** is an Amazon Best-Selling Author and a woman
 of many talents. A published
Author, Life Coach and
Motivational Speaker, Marita
has inspired thousands of people
to overcome adversity with
triumph through faith and
perseverance. While facing
several life changing challenges
herself, Marita had enough faith
to conquer tribulations, coming out victorious. She is best known
for her Christian Fiction novellas and heart felt inspirational books.
Loving God with her whole heart, she has vowed to live a life of
transparency winning souls to Christ with the realness of her
journey and the relatability of her testimony. In March of 2009
Marita published her debut book entitled The Unspoken Walk".
Capturing the true essence of what it means to turn "lemons into
lemonade", she has taken the harsh lessons of life and developed a
plan for successfully living. The Unspoken Walk has afforded
Marita the opportunity to travel all over the country spreading the
wonderful joys of her faith with anyone willing to hear it. That's
where her journey began as a Life Coach. Supporters from across
the country began seeking Mrs. Kinney inspiration and
encouragement. Marita then furthered her education and obtained
her certification for Life Coaching through The Life Purpose
Institute and became Board Certified through The Center for
Credentialing and Education (C.C.E), as an affiliate of the National
Board for Certified Counselors.

Marita proved to be destined to spread God's word like her father,
the late Bishop Westley C Robinson. Marita is also wife of
Comedian, Actor, and Saxophonist, Demoine Kinney. They are the
proud parents of six children. She is also a successful business
woman. Putting herself through college, Marita is a graduate of
Ashworth University, obtaining two degrees, Business

**Sasha**                                        **Marita Kinney**

Administration and Human Resources Management. She has established herself as a source of inspiration, influence, and encouragement to many women. She is also an Advocate for The National Bone Marrow Donor Program, helping to educate minorities on the lack of minority donors and how it affects the community. Marita has been selected by the National Association Of Professional Women as the 2010/2011 "Woman of the Year". She currently writes a column for Hope For Women Magazine and humbly allows God to direct her ministry going wherever the spirit of God leads her.

# LISTEN TO HER TESTIMONY

www.MaritaKinney.com

More Book by Marita

# Snow Series:

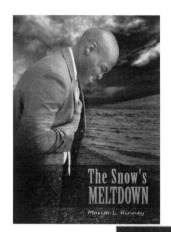

**Sasha**                                          **Marita Kinney**

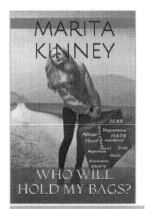

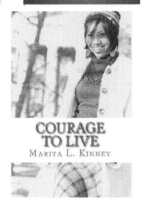

**Sasha**
**Get Connected:**                                              **Marita Kinney**

Just send your email address
by Text Message:

Text
# COURAGE2LIVE
to 22828 to get started.

Made in the USA
San Bernardino, CA
30 March 2014